Barry Pain

Stories and interludes

Barry Pain

Stories and interludes

ISBN/EAN: 9783744748803

Printed in Europe, USA, Canada, Australia, Japan

Cover: Foto ©Andreas Hilbeck / pixelio.de

More available books at **www.hansebooks.com**

STORIES AND INTERLUDES

BY

BARRY PAIN

NEW YORK

HARPER & BROTHERS, FRANKLIN SQUARE

1892

TO

A. N. L.

My thanks are due to the Editors of "The English Illustrated Magazine," "The Illustrated London News," "Black and White," "The Speaker," "The National Observer," "The Granta," and "The Gentlewoman" for permission to reprint several things in this volume.

CONTENTS

STORIES AND INTERLUDES

I

THE GLASS OF SUPREME MOMENTS

LUCAS MORNE sat in his college rooms, when the winter afternoon met the evening, depressed and dull. There were various reasons for his depression. He was beginning to be a little nervous about his health. A week before he had run second in a mile race, the finish of which had been a terrible struggle; ever since then any violent exertion or excitement had brought on symptoms which were painful, and to one who had always been strong, astonishing. He had ·felt them early that afternoon, on coming from the river. Besides, he was discontented with himself. He had had several men in his rooms that afternoon, who were better than he was, men who had enthusiasms and had found them satisfying. Lucas had a moderate devotion to athletics, but no great enthusiasm. Neither had he the finer perceptions. Neither was he a scholar. He was just an ordinary man, and reputed to be a good fellow.

His visitors had drunk his tea, talked of their

1

own enthusiasms, and were now gone. Nothing is so unclean as a used tea-cup; nothing is so cold as toast which has once been hot, and the concrete expression of dejection is crumbs. Even Lucas Morne, who had not the finer perceptions, was dimly conscious that his room had become horrible, and now flung open the window. One of the men—a large, clumsy man—had been smoking mitigated Latakia; and Latakia has a way of rolling itself all round the atmosphere and kicking. Lucas seated himself in his easiest chair.

His rooms were near the chapel, and he could hear the organ. The music and the soft fall of the darkness were soothing; he could hardly see the used tea-cups now; the light from the gas-lamp outside came just a little way into the room, shyly and obliquely.

.   •   •   •   •   •   •

Well, he had not noticed it before, but the fireplace had become a staircase. He felt too lazy to wonder much at this. He would, he thought, have the things all altered back again on the morrow. It would be worth while to sell the staircase, seeing that its steps were fashioned of silver and crystal. Unfortunately he could not see how much there was of it, or whither it led. The first five steps were clear enough; he felt convinced that the workmanship of them was Japanese. But the rest of the staircase was hidden from his sight by a gray veil of mist. He found himself a little angry, in a severe and strictly logical way, that in these days of boasted science we could not prevent a piece of fog, measuring ten feet by seven, from coming in at an open window and sitting down on a staircase which had only just begun to exist, and blotting out all but five steps of it in its very earliest moments. He allowed that it was a beautiful mist; its color changed slowly from gray to rose, and then back again from rose to gray; fire-flies of silver and gold shot through it at intervals; but it was a nuisance, because he wanted to see the rest of the staircase, and it prevented him. Every moment the desire to see more grew stronger. At last he determined to shake off his laziness, and go up the staircase and through the mist into the something beyond. He felt sure that the something beyond would be beautiful—sure with the certainty which has nothing to do with logical conviction.

It seemed to him that it was with an effort that he brought himself to rise from the chair and walk to the foot of that lovely staircase. He hesitated there for a moment or two, and as he did so he heard the sound of footsteps, high up, far away, yet coming nearer and nearer, with light music in the sound of them. Some one was coming down the staircase. He listened eagerly and excitedly. Then through the gray mist came a figure robed in gray.

It was the figure of a woman—young, with wonderful grace in her movements. Her face was veiled, and all that could be seen of her as she paused on the fifth step was the soft, dark hair that reached to her waist, and her arms— white wonders of beauty. The rest was hidden by the gray veil, and the long gray robe, that left, however, their suggestion of classical grace and slenderness. Lucas Morne stood looking at her tremulously. He felt sure, too, that she was looking at him, and that she could see through the folds of the thin gray veil that hid her face. She was the first to speak. Her voice in its gentleness and delicacy was like the voice of a child; it was only afterward that he heard in it the under-thrill which told of more than childhood.

"Why have you not come? I have been waiting for you, you know, up there. And this is the only time," she added.

"I am very sorry," he stammered. "You see—I never knew the staircase was there until to-day. In fact—it seems very stupid of me— but I always thought it was a fireplace. I must have been dreaming, of course. And then this afternoon I thought, or dreamed, that a lot of men came in to see me. Perhaps they really did come; and we got talking, you know——"

"Yes," she said, with the gentlest possible interruption. "I *do* know. There was one man, Fynsale, large, ugly, clumsy, a year your senior. He sat in that chair over there, and sulked, and smoked Latakia. I rather like the smell of Latakia. He especially loves to write or to say some good thing; and at times he can do it. Therefore, you envy him. Then there was Blake. Blake is an athlete, like yourself, but is just a little more successful. Yes, I know you are good, but Blake is very good. You were tried for the 'Varsity—Blake was selected. He and Fynsale both have delight in ability, and you envy both. There was that dissenting little Paul Reece. He is not exactly in your set, but you were at school with him, and so you tolerate him. How good he is, for all his insignificance and social defects! Blake knows that, and kept a guard on his talk this afternoon. He would not offend Paul Reece for worlds. Paul's belief gives him earnestness, his earnestness leads him to self-sacrifice, and self-sacrifice is deep delight to him. You have more ability than Paul Reece, but you cannot reach that kind of enthusiastic happiness, and therefore you envy him. I could say similar things of the other men. It was because they made you vaguely dissatisfied with yourself that they bored you. You take pleasure—a certain pleasure—in athletics, and that pleasure would become an enthusiastic delight if you were a little better at them. Some men could get the enthusiastic delight out of as much as you can do, but your temperament is different. I know you well. You are not easily satisfied. You are not clever, but you are——" She paused, but without any sign of embarrassment.

"What am I?" he asked eagerly. He felt sure that it would be something good, and he was not less vain than other men.

"I do not think I will say—not now."

"But who are you?" His diffidence and stammering had vanished beneath her calm, quiet talk. "You must let me at least ask that. Who are you? And how do you know all this?"

"I am a woman, but not an earth-woman. And the chief difference between us is that I know nearly all the things you do not know, and you do not know nearly all the things that I know. Sometimes I forget your ignorance—do not be angry for a word; there is no other for it, and it is not your fault. I forgot it just now when I asked you why you had not come to me up the staircase of silver and crystal, through the gray veil where the fire-flies live, and into that quiet room beyond. This is the only time; to-morrow it will not be possible. And I have——" Once more she paused.

There was a charm for Lucas Morne in tho things which she did not say. "Your room is dark," she continued, "and I can hardly see you."

"I will light the lamp," said Lucas hurriedly, "and—and won't you let me get you some tea?" He saw, as soon as he had said it, how unspeakably ludicrous this proffer of hospitality was. He almost fancied a smile, a moment's shimmer of little white teeth, beneath the long gray veil. "Or shall I come now—at once?" he added.

"Come now; I will show you the mirror."

"What is that?"

"You will understand when you see it. It is the glass of supreme moments. I shall tell you about it. But come."

She looked graceful, and she suggested the most perfect beauty as she stood there, a slight figure against the background of gray mist, which had grown luminous as the room below grew darker. Lucas Morne went carefully up the five steps, and together they passed through the gray, misty curtain. He was wondering what the face was like which was hidden beneath that veil; would it be possible to induce her to remove the veil? He might, perhaps, lead the conversation thither—delicately and subtly.

"A cousin of mine," he began, "who has

travelled a good deal, once told me that the women of the East——"

"Yes," she said, and her voice and way were so gentle that it hardly seemed like an interruption; "and so do I."

He felt very much anticipated; for a moment he was driven back into the shy and stammering state. There were only a few more steps now, and then they entered through a rosy curtain into a room, which he supposed to be "that quiet room beyond," of which she had spoken.

It was a large room, square in shape. The floor was covered with black and white tiles, with the exception of a small square space in the centre, which looked like silver, and over which a ripple seemed occasionally to pass. She pointed it out to him. "That," she said, "is the glass of supreme moments." There were no windows, and the soft light that filled the room seemed to come from that liquid silver mirror in the centre of the floor. The walls, which were lofty, were hung with curtains of different colors, all subdued, dreamy, reposeful. These colors were repeated in the painting of the ceiling. In a recess at the further end of the room there were seats, low seats on which one could sleep. There was a faint smell of syringa in the air, making it heavy and drowsy. Now and then one heard faintly, as if afar off, the great music of an organ. Could it, he found himself wondering, be the organ of the college chapel? It was restful and pleasant to hear. She drew him to one of the seats in the recess, and once more pointed to the mirror.

"All the ecstasy in the world lies reflected there. The supreme moments of each man's life—the scene, the spoken words—all lie there. Past and present, and future—all are there."

"Shall I be able to see them?"

"If you will."

"And how?"

"Bend over the mirror, and say the name of the man or woman into whose life you wish to see. You only have to want it, and it will appear before your eyes. But there are some lives which have no supreme moments."

· "Commonplace lives?"

"Yes."

Lucas Morne walked to the edge of the mirror and knelt down, looking into it. The ripple passed to and fro over the surface. For a moment he hesitated, doubting for whom he should ask; and then he said in a low voice: "Are there supreme moments in the life of Blake—Vincent Blake, the athlete?" The surface of the mirror suddenly grew still, and in it rose what seemed a living picture.

He could see once more the mile race in which he had been defeated by Blake. It was the third and last lap; and he himself was leading by some twenty yards, for Blake was waiting. There was a vast crowd of spectators, and he could hear every now and then the dull sound of their voices. He saw Vincent Blake slightly quicken his pace, and marked his own plucky attempt to answer it; he saw, too, that he had very little left in him. Gradually Blake drew up, until at a hundred yards from the finish there were not more than five yards between the two runners. Then he noticed his own fresh attempt. There were some fifty yards of desperate fighting, in which neither seemed to gain or lose an inch on the other. The voices of the excited crowd rose to a roar. And then —then Blake had it his own way. He saw himself passed a yard from the tape.

"Blake has always just beaten me," he said savagely as he turned from the mirror.

He went back to his seat. "Tell me," he said; "does that picture really represent the supreme moments of Blake's life?"

"Yes," answered the veiled woman, "he will have nothing quite like the ecstasy which he felt at winning that race. He will marry, and have children, and his married life will be happy, but the happiness will not be so intense. There is an emotion-meter outside this room, you know, which measures such things."

"Now if one wanted to bet on a race," he began. Then he stopped short. He had none of the finer perceptions, but it did not take these to show him that he was becoming a little inappropriate. "I will look again at the mirror," he added after a pause. "I am afraid, though, that all this will make me more discontented with myself."

Once more he looked into the glass of supreme moments. He murmured the name of Paul Reece, the good little dissenter, his old schoolfellow. It was not in the power of accomplishment that Paul Reece excelled Lucas Morne, but only in the goodness and spirituality of his nature. As he looked, once more a picture formed on the surface of the mirror. It was of the future this time.

It was a sombre picture of the interior of a church. Through the open door one saw the snow falling slowly into the dusk of a winter afternoon. Within, before the richly decorated altar, flickered the little ruby flames of hanging lamps. On the walls, dim in the dying light, were painted the stations of the Cross. The fragrance of the incense smoke still lingered in the air. He could see but one figure, bowed, black-robed, before the altar. "And is this Paul Reece—who was a dissenter?" he asked himself, knowing that it was he. Some one was seated at the organ, and the cry of the music was full of appeal, and yet full of peace: "*Agnus Dei, qui tollis peccata mundi!*"

Then the picture died away, and once more the little ripple moved to and fro over the surface of the liquid silver mirror. Lucas went back again to his place. The veiled woman was leaning backward, her small white hands linked together. She did not speak, but he was sure that she was looking at him—looking at him intently. Slowly it came to him that there was in this woman a subtle, mastering attraction which he had never known before. And side by side with this thought there still remained the feeling which had filled him as he witnessed the supreme moments of Paul Reece, a paradoxical feeling which was half restlessness and half peace.

"I do not know if I envy Paul," he said, "but if so, it is not the envy which hurts. I shall never be like him. I can't feel as he does. It's not in me. But this picture did not make me angry as the other did." He looked steadfastly at the graceful, veiled figure, and added in a lower tone: "When I spoke of the travels of my cousin a little while ago—over Palestine and Turkey, and thereabouts, you know—I had meant to lead up to a question, as you saw. I had meant to ask you if you would put away your veil and let me see your face. And there are many things which I want to know about you. May I not stay here by your side and talk?"

"Soon, very soon, I will talk with you, and after that you shall see me. What do think, then, of the glass of supreme moments?"

"It is wonderful. I only feared the sight of exquisite happiness in others would make me more discontented. At first you seemed to think that I was too dissatisfied."

"Do not be deceived. Do not think that these supreme moments are everything; for that life is easiest which is gentle, level, placid, and has no supreme moments. There is a picture in the life of your friend Fynsale which I wish you to see. Look at it in the mirror, and then I shall have something to tell you."

Lucas did as he was bidden. The mirror showed him a wretched, dingy room—sitting-room and bedroom combined—in a lodging-house. At a little rickety table, pushed in front of a very small fire, Fynsale sat writing by lamp-light. The lamp was out of order apparently. The combined smell of lamp and Latakia was poignant. There was a pile of manuscript before him, and on the top of it he was placing the sheet he had just written. Then he rose from his chair, folded his arms on the mantel-piece, and bent down, with his head on his hands, looking into the fire. It was an uncouth attitude of which, Lucas remembered, Fynsale had been particularly fond when he was at college.

When the picture had passed, Lucas looked round, and saw that the veiled woman had left the recess, and was now standing by his side. "I do not understand this," he said. "How can those be the supreme moments in Fynsale's life? He looked poor and shabby, and the room was positively wretched. Where does the ecstasy come in?"

"He has just finished his novel; and he is quite madly in love with it. Some of it is very good, and some of it—from merely physical reasons—is very bad; he was half-starved when he was writing it, and it is not possible to write very well when one is half-starved. But he loves it. I am speaking of all this as if, like the picture of it, it was present; although, of course, it has not happened yet. But I will tell you more. I will show you, in this case at least, what these moments of ecstasy are worth. Some of Fynsale's book, I have said, is very good, and some of it is very bad; but none of it is what people want. He will take it to publisher after publisher, and they will refuse it. After three years it will at last be published, and it will not succeed in the least. And all through these years of failure he will recall from time to time the splendid joy he felt at finishing that book, and how glad he was that he had made it. The thought of that past ecstasy will make the torture all the worse."

"Perhaps, then, after all I should be glad that I am commonplace?" said Lucas.

"It does not always follow, though, that the commonplace people have commonplace lives. There have been men who have been so ordinary that it hurt one to have anything to do with them, and yet the gods have made them come into poetry."

Once more Lucas fancied that a smile with magic in it might be fluttering under that gray veil. Every moment the fascination of this woman, whose face he had not seen, and with whom he had spoken for so short a time, grew stronger on him. He did not know from whence it came, whether it lay in the grace of her figure and her movements, or in the beauty of her long, dark hair, or in the music of her voice, or in that subtle, indefinable way in which she seemed to show him that she cared for him deeply. The room itself, quiet, mystical, restful, dedicated to the ecstasy of the world, had its effect upon his senses. More than ever before he felt himself impressed, tremulous with emotion. He knew that she saw how, in spite of himself, the look of adoration would come into his eyes.

And suddenly she, whom but a moment before he had imagined to be smiling at her own light thoughts, seemed swayed by a more serious impulse.

"You must be comforted, though, and be angry with yourself no longer. For you are *not* commonplace, because you know that you *are* commonplace. It is something to have wanted the right things, although the gods have given you no power to attain them, nor even the wit and words to make your want eloquent." Her voice was deeper, touched with the under-thrill.

"This," he said, "is the second time you have spoken of the gods—and yet we are in the nineteenth century."

"Are we? I am very old and very young. Time is nothing to me; it does not change me. Yesterday in Italy each grave and stream spoke of divinity. *'Non omnis moriar,'* sang one in confidence, *'Non omnis moriar!'* I heard his voice, and now he is passed and gone from the world."

"We read him still," said Lucas Morne, with a little pride. He was not intending to take the classical tripos, but he had with the help of a translation read that ode from which she was quoting. She did not heed his interruption in the least. She went on speaking:

"And to-day in England there is but little which is sacred; yet here, too, my work is seen; and here, too, as they die, they cry, 'I shall not die, but live!'"

"You will think me stupid," said Lucas

Morne, a little bewildered, "but I really do not understand you. I do not follow you. I cannot see to what you refer."

"That is because you do not know who I am. Before the end of to-day I think we shall understand each other well."

There was a moment's pause, and then Lucas Morne spoke again:

"You have told me that even in the lives of commonplace people there are sometimes supreme moments. I had scarcely hoped for them and you have bidden me not to desire them. Shall I—even I—know what ecstasy means?"

"Yes, yes; I think so."

"Then let me see it, as I saw the rest pictured in the mirror." He spoke with some hesitation, his eyes fixed on the tiled floor of the room.

"That need not be," she answered, and she hardly seemed to have perfect control over the tones of her voice now. "That need not be, Lucas Morne, for the supreme moments of your life are here, here and now."

He looked up, suddenly and excitedly. She had flung back the gray veil over her long, dark hair, and stood revealed before him, looking ardently into his eyes. Her face was paler than that of average beauty; the lips, shapely and scarlet, were just parted; but the eyes gave the

2

most wonderful charm.   They were like flames at midnight—not the soft, gray eyes that make men better, but the passionate eyes that make men forget honor, and reason, and everything. She stretched out both hands toward him, impulsively, appealingly.   He grasped them in his own.   His own hands were hot, burning; every nerve in them tingled with excitement. For a moment he held her at arm's-length, looking at her, and said nothing.   At last he found words:

"I knew that you would be like this.   I think that I have loved you all my life.   I wish that I might be with you forever."

There was a strange expression on her face. She did not speak, but she drew him nearer to her.

"Tell me your name," he said.

"Yesterday, where that poet lived—that confident poet—they called me Libitina; and here to-day, they call me Death.   My name matters not, if you love me.   For to you alone have I come thus.   For the rest, I have done my work unseen.   Only in this hour—only in this hour— was it possible."

He had hardly heeded what she said.   He bent down over her face.

"Stay!" she said in a hurried whisper; "if you kiss me you will die."

He smiled triumphantly.   "But I shall die

kissing you," he said.   And so their lips met.
Her lips were scarlet, but they were icy cold.

.   .   .   .

The captain of the football team had just
come out of evening chapel, his gown slung
over his arm, his cap pulled over his eyes, looking good-tempered, and strong, and jolly, but
hardly devotional.   He saw the window of
Morne's rooms open—they were on the ground-
floor—and looked in.   By the glow of the fail-
ing fire he saw what he thought was Lucas
Morne seated in a lounge-chair.   He called to
him, but there was no answer.   "The old idiot's
asleep," he said to himself, as he climbed in at
the window.   "Wake up, old man," he cried,
as he put his hand on the shoulder of Lucas
Morne's body, and swung it forward; "wake
up, old man."

The body rolled forward and fell sideways to
the ground heavily and clumsily.   It lay there
motionless.

II

EXCHANGE

1—Doris

THERE was once a girl-child named Doris who went out skating with her bigger brothers one afternoon over flooded fields in the Fen country. But her brothers played hockey with school-fellows, and Doris skated contentedly enough by herself. She was wearing Bob's skates, which she liked better than her own, and the man had put them on very well indeed. She went from one field through a gap in the hedge into the next, and then on into a third field. There were very few people here, and most of the ice was not swept; all of this was very pleasant to Doris, and made her feel adventurous. It was beautiful, too; and even children unconsciously understand a sunset with those old thin trees trembling black against the crimson disc, and everywhere bits of white brightness on a gray sea of fog. She skated as fast as she could, the wind helping her, feeling strangely and splendidly animated, when quite suddenly . . .

•   •   •   •   •   •   •

But this was not the Fen country. This was the north of Yorkshire. She had been here before on a visit to her cousins. Yonder was the top of Winder; she had climbed it on clear days and seen Morecambe Bay flashing in the distance. But it was night now—almost a black night, and it was very cold for Doris to be wandering over those hills alone. She had an irritating sensation that she had to go somewhere before the dawn came, and that she did not know where or why. It was lonely and awesome. "If I only had somebody to speak to, I shouldn't mind it so much," she said to herself. At once she heard a low voice saying, "Doris! Doris!" and she looked round.

In a recess of the ravine which a ghyll had made for itself as it leaped from the cold purity of a hill-top to the warm humanity of a village in the valley—a village no better than it should have been—a small fire of sticks was smouldering. Doris could just see that the person crouched in front of the fire—the person who had called her by her name—was an old, haggard woman, with her chin resting on her knees.

"Tell me, old woman," Doris said almost angrily, "what does this all mean? I was at Lingay Fen skating, and now I am wandering over the Yorkshire hills. It has changed from afternoon to night——"

"It generally does," said the old woman in a chilly, unemphatic way. Doris stamped her foot impatiently. "I mean that it has changed quite suddenly. Just a moment ago, too, I felt quite certain that I had to go somewhere, and I had forgotten where. Now I don't think I have to go anywhere."

"No—you have arrived," said the old woman softly.

At that moment a dry twig burst into flame, and lit up the old woman's face and figure for a second. She was hideous enough; her face was thin and yellow; her cavernous eyes sparkled to the momentary flicker. Her dress and cloak were torn and faded, but they had been bright scarlet.

"You naturally ask why," she continued, "because you are young and have not yet learned the uselessness of it. What has just happened to you seems very meaningless and foolish, but it is not more meaningless and foolish than the rest of things. It is all a poor sort of game, you know. Explain? No, I shall not explain; but it was I who brought you here. Sit down by me under the night sky, and watch."

"No, I will not," said Doris, and walked away. She took about ten paces away, and then came back again and did the very thing which she said she would not do. She sat down by the old woman, and was a little angry because she could not help doing it. Then she began to grumble at the fire. "That's not half a fire," she said; "it just smoulders and makes smoke. I will show you what you ought to do. You put on some fresh sticks—so. Then you put your mouth quite close to the embers, and blow and keep—on—blowing. There!" She had fitted her actions to her words, and now a bright flame leaped out. It shone all over, on her dark hair and dark bright eyes, and on the gray furs of her dress. It shone, too, on the old woman, who was smiling an ugly, half-suppressed smile.

"Doris," said the old woman, "leave the fire alone. I do not want flame. I only want it to stream forth smoke."

"But why?"

"See now—there." The old woman made a downward gesture with both hands, and the flame sank obediently down again, giving place to a quick yield of black smoke. "Look at the smoke, Doris. That is what you have to watch." There was a little more energy in the old, quavering voice now.

Doris did as she was told; but suddenly she stopped and cried, half-frightened, "There are faces in it!"

"Yes, yes," said the old woman, almost eagerly; "and there are pictures of the future

in it—of the future as it will be unless I alter
it this night. I alone can alter it, you know.
Are you not glad now that you came?"

"It is something like fortune-telling; did you
ever have your fortune told?"

"No, I never did," replied the old woman.
Her smile was very ugly indeed.

"But how shall I know that it's true?"

"Why, you *do* know."

That was the strangest part of it. Doris felt
certain without having a reason that she could
give for it. "Show me my future," she said
breathlessly.

"Watch the smoke, then."

So she watched, and picture followed picture.
At the first of them she made some little exclama-
tion. "Ah!" she cried, "that is a splendid
dress; and I *do* like those shoes. I wish I
might have long dresses now—I'm sure I'm old
enough; and I want to have my hair done up
the proper way, but——" She stopped suddenly, because the picture had changed. "I
look much prettier in this one," she said. "I
have been dancing, I think, from the dress, and
because I seem a little out of breath. There is
a man with me, and now he—no, no! I would
not. I should hate it. That picture cannot
be right!" The third picture represented her
marriage with great splendor. "Well," she
said, "I do not mind that so much—just stand-

ing up and wearing a beautiful veil. But I
don't want to be married at all. I like skating
ever so much better."

There was a faint sound of laughter, muffled
and bitter, from the old woman. "You like
skating?" she said. "Where are your skates,
then, Doris?" Doris looked for them, but could
not find them, and this distressed her. "Oh,
what *shall* I do? They were not my skates;
they were Bob's."

"Who is Bob?"

"Bob is my smallest brother—ever so much
younger than I am; he's my favorite brother,
too. He's got red hair, but he's a pretty
boy."

"He must be a milksop if he can't skate."

"He *can* skate. He can do the outside edge
backward; he skates better than any of my
three big brothers."

"Well, well—it's a pity that he's stupid,
though."

"Stupid? Do you know why he lent me his
skates? Because he was going to write a story
this afternoon, and he's going to put me in it.
Bob can do almost anything. He's wonderful.
When he grows up he'll very likely write a
whole book, he says."

"Look at his future—Bob's future—in the
smoke," said the old woman grimly, heaping on
more sticks.

Doris looked reluctantly. The pictures came flashing past one after the other. Some she could not altogether understand, for she knew nothing of the vices of young men; but they were vaguely terrible. But even a child could understand the last picture of all. It was awful and vivid. She almost fancied that she could hear the report of the pistol, and the dim thud as the body fell awkwardly on the floor.

"You needn't cry," said the old woman, as Doris burst into tears.

"Oh! Bob is so splendid," sobbed Doris. "Don't let it be like that. Do alter it. You don't know him or you would change it. You said you could. I'll give you everything I've got if you'll stop it somehow."

"Will you give me your beauty—your youth— your life?"

"Oh, willingly—everything!"

"I want none of them—none of them," said the old woman fiercely and quickly. "But I want something else. Give it me, and I will alter it as you wish." She stretched out a lean finger and tapped Doris' forehead, and whispered a few words in her ear.

Doris turned white enough, but she nodded assent. "Then it will alter my future, too," she said with a little gasp.

"It will alter the future of everybody in the

world — indirectly and in some cases very slightly. But you will give it me? "

"Yes, yes." She paused a moment, and then added a torrent of questions: "Old woman, who are you? Why are you dressed in scarlet? Why did you have me brought here? I should like it to turn out to be a dream. Oh! why do you want it? Why are you so horribly—horribly cruel? "

But the old woman, and the fire, and the great dark hills grew dim and indistinct; and there was no answer.

. . . .

The two old men—one with a medical, the other with a military air—came slowly down the broad staircase from the bedrooms without speaking. The little red-headed boy was waiting for them as usual. "Is Doris any better, papa? " he asked eagerly. " Will she live? "

It was no good to keep it from him; he would have to know sooner or later.

"Yes, Bob," said the colonel, "she will live. But the—the injury to her head has——" He stopped with a gulping sound in his voice. The boy looked up at him wistfully with a scared face.

"Don't, colonel," said the doctor; "you'd better leave it to me. I will tell the boy."

2—MAJOR GUNNICAL

NOBODY ever denied in my presence that Major Gunnical was a capital shot and a good fellow. He went straight, and it was always imputed to him for righteousness. But the other day the only man of the world with whom I am acquainted accused the major of want of taste, and based his accusation on the fact that he took the liberty of dying in the country-house of a friend, not having been invited for that purpose. I might have pointed out that Major Gunnical knew Sir Charles quite well enough to take a liberty which would have been unpardonable in a casual guest; I might have added that it was one of those accidents which may happen to any man, and that it was unintentional and unforeseen on the major's part. But I prefer to give the facts of the case, which seem to me to explain everything.

On the evening which opened the night of his death, Major Gunnical had gone upstairs to dress sooner than the rest of them. He stood in his bedroom with his back to the fire, well knowing that if the back be warm the whole body is warm also. He was half-afraid that he had caught a chill, and chills affected him. There was nothing in his appearance to tell you that his heart was wrong. His body was large and muscular, and he looked a strong man.

His hair had only just begun to get a little gray. His complexion was pale, but it had been tanned by hot suns and seemed clear and healthy. His eyes were thoughtful gray eyes—quite out of keeping with the active look of the man. His best point was his simple directness; he could do right things, even when they were not easy, without thinking of them at the time or afterward. His worst point was his temper, which broke loose occasionally. At the present moment he was thinking about himself, which was not a usual occurrence with Major Gunnical, and his thoughts were depressing; so he tried to dismiss them. "It's all nervousness and too much tobacco," he thought to himself; "but I will go up to town to-morrow and let old Peterson prescribe for me. I shall be all right in a day—probably only liver—no exercise, thanks to this cursed frost. Oh, yes, it's just liver—nothing else."

He paused once when he was fastening his collar, and said slowly and distinctly, "Damn presentiments." But he was not able to shake off a feeling of quietness: a desire to be at peace with men and a tendency to look at the sad side of things. When he got downstairs he found only one man already in the drawing-room—a man called Kenneth, who wrote. Now there was a certain disagreement between Kenneth and the major. In the smoking-room the night before, the major had expressed his sincere admiration for a certain story of soldier life by a new writer, and Kenneth had explained to him that this admiration was wrong, because the story was not at all well constructed.

"I own," he had said, "that it takes a critic to see the faults of the technique." This was a little vain of Kenneth. "Yes," said the major hotly, "and it takes a *man* to feel the merits of the story." This was a little rude of the major, for Kenneth was obviously an effeminate person. Kenneth put up his eye-glasses and looked at the major curiously. "Don't be so damnably affected," said the major. Then Sir Charles had interposed lazily.

Consequently, when the major entered the drawing-room Kenneth at once began to assume more dignity than Providence had made him able to carry easily. The major walked up to him and held out one hand. "Look here, Kenneth," he said, "I'm an old fool, and always thinking I know another man's business as well as my own. I'd no right to question your opinion last night and make an angry ass of myself. I'm sorry." Kenneth's dignity came down heavily, and he took the major's hand at once. For a fortnight he loved him, and then he told publicly the story of how he had gone to the major and forced him to apologize. For there is a combination of imagination and vanity which nothing — not even kindness—can kill.

The major was very dull at dinner, but when his host's two children came in afterward, they seemed to find him very satisfactory. The major loved children. He did not stop very long in the smoking-room that night. He wanted badly to be alone.

For some time after he had gone to bed he lay awake thinking. Maude, his host's elder daughter, reminded him in appearance of his own niece Doris. It seemed hard that Maude should be so bright and happy, and that Doris —owing to a skating accident—should be condemned to lose all her brightness, and her flow of talk, and her power to understand. Yet Doris never seemed actually unhappy; her eyes were vacant, as if the light behind them had gone out, but she did not seem to be suffering. During the first part of her illness she had babbled about some woman, an old woman dressed in scarlet, who frightened her.

Thus thinking, the major fell asleep. It was long past midnight when he opened his eyes and saw a figure of a woman standing on the hearth-rug, and stretching yellow hands like claws toward the remnant of the fire. It startled him, but he did not want to wake up the rest of the house.

"What are you doing in my room?" he said in a rapid whisper.

The old woman turned round. He could hardly see her face, but the flicker of the fire showed him that she was dressed in rags of faded scarlet. Her voice was very gentle and low.

"Awake? Are you awake? I made a little noise to wake you on purpose. But generally they go on sleeping when I come. I am the scarlet woman of whom Doris spoke. She has been taken."

"Dead? A merciful deliverance."

"No, she is not delivered yet. She has to go through life again in a lower form before she is delivered. I hate her. I will see that she is unhappy again before she is delivered."

"Why does this all seem real instead of seeming fantastic and absurd — as it ought to?"

"Because it *is* real; but they always ask me that, all those who see me. Doris shall become a caged bird, I think—one of those who are driven nearly mad by captivity and yet are so strong that they die slowly."

"You can't do that," said the major quickly.

"You know I can, and you know I shall," replied the old woman in the same soft whisper. "I need not argue, or prove, or do anything of that kind. When I speak men *know* that all is as I say; but they do not often hear me, because they are nearly always asleep when I come."

"Where is Doris now?"

"She waits in dreamland, where nothing is real, until I get my opportunity, and she is born once more, and caught, and caged, and tortured."

As she said this she seemed to grow a little more excited; and, as if in sympathy with her, the fire suddenly burned up more brightly, and showed her horrible, lean face, and deep, leering eyes.

"That's cruel," said the major. "And what shall I be when I die?"

"You will not have a bad time," she said, grinning. "You shall be a dear little white lamb that lives an hour and then is delivered. You will die to-night, by the way. But Doris shall beat her heart out against bars, because I hate her. You will see one another in dreamland, while you are waiting until I get the two right opportunities."

An idea occurred to the major. "Change us, Doris and myself."

The old woman trembled with agitation, and her voice rose shrilly. "I will not! I will not!" she cried.

But something bright and sure, like a steady light, seemed to fill the man's mind. "But you

3

will—you cannot help it," he answered very quietly.

The old woman strode quickly across the room, her face aflame with rage, and touched him on the heart. He fell backward, and did not speak any more.

"I must always come when they are asleep in future," said the old woman, as she went back to the fire. "It is too much to risk—I have lost by Doris and this man." There was a long pause. "But I will torture him even more than I would have tortured Doris," she whispered gently to the fire.

. . . .

Two months afterward a white lamb was born, in a sheltered place, on a grassy fell. And in an hour it died.

And on the same day a certain bird-catcher, resident in Whitechapel, went out early and had luck.

3—Doris in the Hereafter

THE release had come at last. To Doris it was an exquisite release; the years spent in darkness were over; the short, mystical period which followed her death was over; her spirit went out into the moonlit night—white, naked, beautiful. She could remember but little consciously of her earth-life. She had suffered—

she could recollect that, and she had spoken with a grim woman—an old woman dressed in rags of faded scarlet. She did not recollect what had been said, but she knew that it had been the beginning of the darkness which had fallen on her mind. Of her death she knew nothing; of a short strange time after her death she knew a little, dimly and vaguely.

She was free, and it was enough for her. It seemed to her that she still kept the body which had been called Doris during its earth-life, but that now it was light as the air, stronger than before, and far more beautiful. She stood, a childish figure, graceful and erect, on a shred of dark cloud which a steady night wind blew past the hill-tops and over the valley. Below her she could see the flooded river, angry with its old stone bridges, crying itself to sleep in long, still reaches, with the mists rising white all about it. She saw, too, much that the living do not see. In a lonely cottage, low and roughly built, some young spring flowers had just died; she saw their souls—their fragrance, as she had been used to call it—pass upward; and as they passed they changed and became a handful of ghost-lilies in the garden-land of dreams. And all night long she went on her way, seeing beautiful things. She could never be tired any more; and the rain and the dew did not hurt her; and the cold wind did not seem cold to her.

And when the morning came, a little baby breeze came up to her with a message. It was so young and forgetful that it had not got the exact words of the message. But it remembered the drift of it. "He said you were to go and look for sorrows," it whispered in her ear. It lingered for a moment, playing with her hair, and then it went down below and tried to blow a dandelion clock. And not being strong enough, it sat down and sulked; for it had not yet learned that the only things worth doing are the things one cannot do.

Then Doris went on about her work, very happy, singing little songs that she remembered. And first of all she went to a great house where a proud and beautiful lady lived. But the proud lady sat huddled up and quite undignified in her own room, crying till her nose was red and she was not pleasant to see. And all because some one or other—I think it was her husband—was dead, and was going to be forever happy! Doris laughed contemptuously, and passed on.

She next went to a nursery where there was a little freckled girl with sandy hair. And the little girl was unhappy because of a bad accident to a ninepenny doll, which was her most intimate friend. There was a small hole in the doll's neck and a possible escape of sawdust. It was only by holding the doll wrong way up and shaking it that you could make the sawdust come out; and the little girl did not want the sawdust to come out at all, for it caused her agony when it came out; and yet she held the doll upside down and shook it. For this was the kind of girl that, when she grows up, becomes a woman. Doris was sorry for her, and whispered in her ear, "You had better get a little piece of stamp-paper and stick it over the hole in the doll's neck—but it won't last long." The child thought Doris was a beautiful idea, and went radiantly to the study and opened the despatch-box. There was no stamp-paper. There was one penny stamp, and she knew that it was wicked to take it. So she compromised—which was feminine of her—and tore the stamp in two and only took half of it. Then she went back to the nursery, and fixed the half-stamp as Doris had suggested. Doris, who had watched her, was horrified. "You ought not to have taken that stamp," she said to her. "You had better confess what you have done, and say that you do not wish to tell a lie." Then the little girl supposed Doris was conscience—for, of course, Doris was invisible—and did not think quite so much of her. Neither did she confess. Doris was not very unhappy about it, knowing that children are always forgiven and occasionally forgotten.

She saw many other sorrows and she thought

very little of them. People, she perceived, always exaggerated the importance of death, and money, and love. Yet she saw a wind—a venomous wind—snap the stalk of the very loveliest daffodil, and nobody wore black clothes for it, or had sherry-and-biscuits, or showed any of the signs of sorrow. She had only been for a few hours in the Hereafter, and yet she already felt herself to be out of touch with humanity.

And it happened that she came to a great dirty city, and she stopped where a cage of wicker-work was hung outside a grimy shop in a grimy street. There were several things in the cage: a yellow glass for water with no water in it; a blue glass for seed with no seed in it; something which had once been a turf and now looked like a badly cooked brick; and something which panted on the floor of the cage in the corner—it was all that was left of a bird, a soaring bird that loved the upper air and the sunlight, but was now reduced to plain dying and high thinking. Now none of the other sorrowful persons had seen Doris; but the bird saw her and called to her, but she did not understand the language. She went into the shop and whispered to the man in charge, "Your bird outside wants attention; it's ill."

"Bless my soul! and I gave a shilling for it!" So he took the bird some water and something

to eat which was not good for it. The bird
chirped. "It knows me and loves me already,"
said the man. It was really saying, "Would
you kindly wring my neck, and end this?"

"I am sorry for it," said Doris, as she passed
on. "I am glad I was never a pet." She
would have been more sorry if she had known
all the history of that bird.

A MAN AND A GOD

"᾿Εγὼ δὲ λιμῷ ἀπόλλυμαι."

I HUNGER and am not satisfied:
Because I am small, and the world is wide;
And the world is one, and the stars are sand,
Flung right out by a careless hand
Into the darkness to slide and slide;
And all the darkness is one small blot
That He who made it regardeth not.
He hath nor sorrow, nor joy, nor pride,
And His face is set as it were of stone;
He worked, and he letteth the work alone;
And none are above Him and none beside.

The dead leaf blown from the dying tree,
The great ship wrecked in a cruel sea,
The creeping things that the cart-wheels crush,
The ruined star in its downward rush—
Alike to Him all these things be,
And the darkness is as the day's full light,
Ever and ever, by day and night,   ·
He sits alone, and His great eyes see
A million worlds in their courses turn;
Yet like a flame the deep looks burn
Even in this small heart of me.

He thought me, and He let me go;
He thought a man and it was so.
For He thinketh all and there liveth naught
That came not first from out God's thought;
Then we are left—to die or grow,
He has forgotten us all by now,
And stony swoon on His stony brow
Lies, and His breath is strong and slow.
He sees, and recks not what He sees,
And never it moveth His frozen ease
That we cry, and die, and rot below.

Yet the far hills, that snow makes white,
Stretch Godward, longing for His light;
And all last night the winds outpoured
Their rhythmic Glory to the Lord—
I listened longingly last night.
We hunger and are not satisfied;
All the worlds and the darkness wide,
Every depth and every height,
Longing to be in God again.
And hunger is hunger, and longing vain,
And man is nothing, and God is right.

III

RURAL SIMPLICITY

My Dearest Clara:—I am going to write you a long letter. There is just a little news to tell you, and I want to talk about something I could not possibly discuss with any one else. You are only a few years older than I am, and yet you know so much more about things. I feel sure that if you advise me at all, you will advise me well. You have read so many more novels and stories than I have, that you understand human nature much better. And you are so sympathetic too. I have often thought it very sad that at the age of twenty-five you should have decided that you can never love again; but I know that you do take the warmest and deepest interest in the love-stories of others, and there is no one to whom I could more readily tell all the secrets of my heart. You must not imagine that I have any love-story or any secrets of that kind to tell you now.

On the contrary, I have just realized that you are quite right about my cousin Tom, and that I can never, never love him at all. Every word that you said about him was true: mere good looks, good nature, and a partiality for athletics are *not* enough; I can see now how right you were when you told me that "one wants the wonderful insight and sympathy that can understand the delicacies and simplicities of a young girl's soul"—I think that is the most beautiful sentence in your last dear letter. And it is *so* true! It is just a little difficult for me, because Tom is living at the rectory until he goes up to Cambridge in October, and although he spends a good deal of his time in the study with papa, working for his examination, he does get a good many opportunities of seeing me. He really behaves just as if I had encouraged him; and he seems almost to expect me to fall in love with him. I like him well enough, but it would be absurd to think about loving him. I did that only before I had the benefit of your wise advice, my dear Clara.

And now I must tell you a little news. Do you remember how you used to rave about " The Long Dream "? Of course you do, because in your last letter you speak of the book again, and say what a consolation it has been to you in your great trouble. You give me, too, a sketch of what you imagine the author, Mr. Merle,

must be like. What will you say when I tell
you that for the last fortnight Mr. Merle has·
been living at Carleston, and that I have seen
him constantly? It's true. Oh!

You were not quite right in your imaginary
description of him. You said that you thought
the author of " The Long Dream" would be " tall
and dark, with flashing eyes and a complexion
like cream with the faintest suspicion of coffee
in it." He really has rather a roundish face,
a fresh color, and fair hair which is generally
rather untidy. I think his eyes are gray; but
I have not been near enough to see properly.
You were quite right in thinking that he would
be tall, however. What made you guess that?
In dress he is just like any other man.

Mr. Merle's father and mine were at college
together, it turns out; so naturally we have seen
a good deal of him. He has dined here twice
and been to tennis several times. He plays
better than Tom. He has got rooms at an old
farm-house, and will perhaps stay for another
month, he says. Papa is delighted with him,
and so is Aunt Mary; Tom does not like him
so much, and says that he is conceited. This
is utterly untrue; he is really quite unaffected,
and very good-tempered. He does not mind
talking about his books; I told him last night
that I loved " The Long Dream," and it seemed
to please him. Was I wrong? Tom behaves

very badly, I am sorry to say, and cannot even keep his temper when Mr. Merle beats him at tennis. I think a boy of eighteen ought to know better, and I told him so. Then he got angry, and said a perfectly outrageous thing—a thing for which there is not the slightest foundation, which no amount of intimacy could have justified him in saying. I would not speak to him all the rest of that day; and I have now told him that if he dares even to hint at such a thing again, I will never speak to him any more at all. I cannot think what has come over poor Tom lately; he used to be all right, but now he is horrible. He seems to have completely changed during the last fortnight. He said the other day that Mr. Merle was an atheist. I told him that, even if it were true, such a charge would come very badly from him, because, as you know, on fine mornings Tom is rather given to shirking church; and I pointed out to him that Mr. Merle had been to church twice on each of the Sundays that he has been here—he sits just opposite to our pew—and that he must have listened to papa's sermons, because he talked to papa about them afterward. Tom had no reason whatever to offer for saying so; except that he had been told that most authors were atheists. I asked him how about St. Paul? which of course he couldn't answer.

I do wish that Tom could manage to behave

a little more as Charles Leader, Mrs. Leader's eldest son, did. I saw a good deal of him some time ago, and he asked me to marry him, you know, shortly after Tom's arrival here. He had simply misunderstood my manner to him; but when I told him his mistake, he never reproached me at all; he has left the village and never troubled me since. I wish Tom would go away too. It is so indelicate of him to keep on caring for me when I have stopped caring for him.

You must not think that, when I said Mr. Merle's face was roundish, that I meant it in a disparaging way at all. He is very good-looking; he has that appearance of nobility and strength which I so much admire in a man. He makes every one like him, except Tom. I wish I could give you a better idea of his personal appearance, but there really is no one we know who could be compared with him for a moment. He likes music; I sang two or three songs for him in the drawing-room the last time he dined here. He has a strange way of looking at one sometimes, as if he were thirsty. It is very interesting to talk to him; he has just come from London, you see, and has heaps of things to tell us. One hears so little in this benighted village. We are going to have tea at his rooms in the farm-house this afternoon, which will be splendid. Tom says he shall not go. I shall meet him again in the evening at Mrs. Leader's. Please write soon to me, dearest Clara, and tell me what to do.

Ever your most loving friend,

MILLICENT MARSHE.

P. S.—His other names are Cecil Vanstoun. He only puts the initials, you know, on the title-page of his book. I forgot to say that I think I like him very much—very much indeed. I have begun to keep a diary; you suggested it some time ago.

2—A LETTER FROM CECIL VANSTOUN MERLE TO JOHN DUNHAM, FELLOW OF SIDNEY COLLEGE, CAMBRIDGE, SEPTEMBER 3D

DEAR JACK:—No, I am not going to give you a humorous and epigrammatic account of the aborigines of Carleston, and the way they treat the unusual apparition of a live Londoner. That kind of thing has been done too often and too badly. Besides, I may possibly be an author, but I am certainly a man of business. I couldn't send you, free, in a letter that which might be printed and purchased. It would offend your natural delicacy; at any rate it ought to; I might as well send you a couple of guineas at once as amusement to that amount. And lastly, what is the use of a friend if we may not be very dull with him? We keep our brilliant side for the comparative stranger, or sell it to the positive editor; we use it to make an impression or a livelihood; we don't waste it on friends.

Well, as you know, I came down here from London about a fortnight ago, sick of the season, overworked, eagerly desiring to be alone, and dumb, and idle, and to drink new milk. I am already somewhat refreshed. I have drunk the new milk; I have stretched myself on the grass in the sun, and smoked many pipes, and become an object of derision to my landlady by reason of my laziness; I do not think she ever had a lodger who did less and enjoyed it more; and if I have not been absolutely dumb, I can at least guarantee that I have said nothing which would be worth repetition. I like this village; there's an indefinable air of goodness and rural simplicity about it. My rooms are not exactly artistic, of course, but everything is spotlessly clean. Why is bad Berlin wool-work on the sofa always accompanied by minatory texts on the walls? It is a pity that you restrict yourself to answering academical questions and I restrict myself to asking the other kind. The rooms do very well; I have imported a good piano, which is rather luxurious of me, I suppose.

But I have not been alone. When I decided, rather in a hurry, to take these rooms and come to Carleston for a couple of months or so, I neglected to inquire who was the village parson. He is the Rev. Hubert Marshe, and was at Trinity with my father. They were friends, and consequently I have been up to the rectory a good deal. He is a man of some culture, has a touch of bibliomania, is gentle in everything but his orthodoxy, and is really loved by every one in the village. His wife died six years ago, and an unmarried sister, Mary Marshe, keeps house for him. She is rather a prim old lady, and insists on all the small points, but she has as sweet a disposition as her brother. A nephew of his is stopping in the house, and is supposed to be reading for the little-go with the rector. He seems to occupy most of his time with adoring the rector's only child Millicent, a girl of seventeen. He himself is not a bad fellow altogether, but rather a cub. Cambridge will improve him.

I went to dine last night with a Mrs. Leader, a widow who has a big house here, but who formerly lived in Cornwall. I had met her at the rectory. By the way, whenever the rector's nephew, Tom, gets very angry with the rector's daughter, Millicent—which happens sometimes, because he is as unreasonable as most adorers— he always talks to her about this Mrs. Leader's elder son, who is now away from home. He does this simply to annoy her—a fact which I had in my mind when I said he was rather a

4

cub. However, that's none of my business. It was rather a pleasant dinner. Mrs. Leader has that shade of gentle Puritanism in her which one still finds occasionally in the inhabitants of English villages. It is the old Puritanism with charity added. She is hard on herself and indulgent to the rest of the world. There are some good people still alive, my dear Jack, but one does not as a rule meet them in London. For real goodness and simplicity one must come to the country. I had a long talk with Mrs. Leader about her elder son Charles, whom she worships, and, curiously enough, I had another talk with Miss Marshe on the same subject later in the evening. She implied, in that vague and delicate way which comes to girls by instinct, that Charles Leader had asked her to marry him, and that she had refused him. She did not say either of these things directly, but she talked as if I knew them, until I actually did know them, and altogether—well, I am going to stop these uninteresting details and come to the main point. I had not meant to tell you, but I find that I must. You may have guessed it already—you are rather clever at such things. I take back all that I have ever said about women. I had never met the perfect woman before, but I have met her now. I love Millicent Marshe, and I am going to ask her to marry me.

At least, I am not sure whether I shall ask her to marry me or not. I am not yet sure whether she cares for her cousin Tom. I rather gathered from a hint that her aunt let fall that a marriage between these two was not unlikely. If she really cares for Tom, of course I shall not annoy her by my interference. You must not misunderstand me when I say that she is perfect. I do not mean that her attainments—her intellectual attainments—are better than those of all other women. I have not entirely lost my critical faculty. I can see, for instance, that her playing is slipshod, and her singing only shows the average drawing-room quality. Very likely she was not well taught. What I meant rather was that she was quite unspoiled. I feel sure that she has never given one sentimental thought to a man in her life. There are girls in town who have a hideous practice of writing morbid confidences to each other about men they have met. She would never do that. She is quite incapable, too, of fickleness. She will love once and love always. But at present she has never thought of love and marriage. She is the perfect, virginal type—fresh and untainted as a fragrant wild-flower in one of the hedge-rows here; and yet a strange, unconscious, delicate instinct keeps her from all mistakes— she would never let a man believe that she cared for him if she did not. This Charles

Leader, who, I have told you, asked her to
marry him, must have been an idiot to have
thought that he had a chance. She would never
lead a man on unless she meant to marry him.
She has lived all her days in this country village, far away from the vulgar flirtations and
sickly sentimentalities of London. She is a
white soul, framed in a lovely body. I could
write pages about her beauty, Jack, but I fear
you would only laugh at me. She has dark
hair, and brown, faithful eyes, and a young
rosebud of a mouth that—what am I doing?—I
who have hated sentimentality all my days!
Yes, you may laugh at me as much as you like.
I don't mind. I suppose it will all be over
soon, for I am afraid that it is for Tom, not for
me, that she cares. I have studied character
all my life, and I do not think I can be mistaken.

Briefly, my plan is this. I shall observe as
closely as possible during the next few days.
If she seems to favor Tom, I shall go away and
trouble her no more. If she seems to favor me,
I shall propose to her. I feel absolutely sure
that she would never mislead either Tom or
myself. You will tell me that I am wanting
in pluck, but I do not think so. It would be
foolhardiness to propose to her if she obviously
cared for Tom; and it would also be, probably,
very offensive to her. I do not allow myself to

hope much, and yet at times hopes will force
their way in, and I picture happiness.

That is my plan of campaign. Cambridge
is quite desolate just now, I suppose. Why do
you stop? I had a good deal to tell you about
a book that I am planning, but I've taken up
all my space with my account of Millicent
Marshe. You may be as amused as you please,
but it's terribly serious with me, and I have no
notion how it will all end.

Ever yours,
CECIL VANSTOUN MERLE.

3—EXTRACTS FROM THE DIARY OF MILLICENT MARSHE

September 3d.—Oh! oh! oh! I wish I could
understand myself. I wish I knew what I was
doing. I wrote a long letter to Clara about Mr.
Merle this morning. I went to his rooms with
the others this afternoon. I met him at dinner
this evening at Mrs. Leader's. I am immensely
interested in him, but I am not quite sure that
I love him; what is much worse is that I am
by no means sure that he loves me. Tom
walked back with me from the Leaders' to the
vicarage, and I thought that he did not seem to
care for me as much as he once did. Of course,
that was just what I wanted, for I can never
marry Tom; but it pained me to see that he
could be so fickle and forget so easily. So I

made a sort of appeal to his better nature, to see
if he really had forgotten; and now I am afraid
that he will think I was encouraging him.   I
do not believe Charles Leader has ever forgotten
me.   I only wish that he would, except that it
would rather lessen my high opinion of him.
I do so *hate* fickleness.   I like simplicity and
constancy.

Mr. Merle is very brilliant.   He has had a
piano sent down here from London, and I sang
" Love's Rapturous Sorrow " to him this afternoon at his rooms; I thought that he might
have thanked me rather more warmly.   When
I had finished, Aunt Mary asked him if he
played, and he said that he did, a little.   I was
rather surprised at this, because it had never
occurred to me that any men, except profes-
sionals, played the piano at all.   He consented
to play at once and asked me what I should like.
I suggested the " Pathétique Sonata," because I
can never make the rondo go right, and I wanted
to see if he could.   " You're right," he said, as
he sat down at the piano.   " The school-girls
have got at that terribly, but they will never
make me stop liking it.   Didn't you find that
in the days when you were at school? "   He did
not wait for me to reply, but began at once.   He
played it all through without notes magnifi-
cently.   He would not play any more, and he
would not sing, although he confessed that he

sang "a little." I wish that I had known all this before I sang those drawing-room songs to him. He must have *hated* them, and probably he hates me in consequence. I think that if he had possessed perfect taste he would not have played quite so well—he would have seen that it was a sort of reproach to me. Besides, I thought that he had got the piano simply for my pleasure, and now it appears that he got it entirely for his own. Still I do not think that he *meant* to be selfish. Men as a rule have very little tact. Yet, I don't know—I fancy that I should not have liked him so well if he had been less brilliant. I cannot help thinking about the power he holds. His book is read everywhere and quoted everywhere. It is admired by the very best critics, and yet I am almost sure that he was pleased when I told him that I loved it. I like to feel that he can do things which are beyond other men, but I do wish he would be a little—how shall I write it? —a little more decided. · He leaves me uncertain.

Charles Leader never did that. Whenever I go to Mrs. Leader's I always find a certain train of thoughts—tender and sorrowful—start up in my brain about Charlie, as I called him then. Charlie was always quite decided. But *so* mistaken! Tom never left me in doubt, either. He's mistaken, too.

September 4th.—I have just had a long letter from my dear Clara, answering the letter
which I sent the day before yesterday. I have
no notion how she arrived at the conclusion, but
this is it:

" Unconsciously perhaps, you are very much
in love with Cecil Vanstoun Merle."

What magic there is in those words! I
think I have read them over a hundred times,
and it makes me tremble to write them down.
I cannot imagine how she guessed it. She
must have great insight in these things, or she
would never have discovered my feelings from
my letter. I had hardly guessed them myself.
Well, this is my own diary, and no one but myself will ever read it; so I will write down my
confession. I love Cecil Vanstoun Merle. I
love him more than any one or anything in the
whole world. I could never, never, never love
any one else. And he has not yet shown me
plainly that he loves me. Consequently, I have
no right to love him.

I *won't* love him.

I can't help loving him.

I should like just to sit down and cry forever
and ever. I am very unhappy. And yet I am
not sure that I shall not in the end be very
happy indeed, if I only follow the plan which
dear Clara has made out for me—the plan of
campaign, she calls it. She is so wise, and

she has had experience. This is what she says:

"You know, my dear Millicent, that I myself have loved and lost. I was then in the first bloom of my girlhood, young, guileless, tender-hearted, beautiful, some said. I never attempted to conceal my passion, *and that was why I lost him*. Men only care to win what is difficult to win. Especially is this the case with men of the bold and intensely masculine physique that you describe in Cecil Merle. An obstacle is an allurement to such men. I am convinced that if you show Cecil Merle that you care for him, he will at once lose any love that he may have for you. If, on the other hand, you show a marked preference for your cousin, and if Cecil cares in the least degree for you now, he will care a thousandfold more then, and you may count on a proposal from him before he leaves Carleston. Besides, this is the only truly maidenly course to pursue; my own conduct was unwise. I was blinded by love, and I have paid the debt in a life-long sorrow."

I almost think that she is right. There may, perhaps, be a little difficulty with Tom. A very little encouragement always encourages Tom so very much. He may not see the true motives for my conduct; and even if he saw them he might be selfish. Of course, if he really loved me, it would be a pleasure to him to add to my

happiness; and he would be adding to my happiness if he helped me to win Mr. Merle—I mean
if he helped to give Mr. Merle an opportunity
of winning me.   Perhaps that is the way that
I ought to look at it.   Besides, as Clara points
out, if Tom presumes too far, I can always tell
him that he is insulting me.   Yes, I must for a
few days try Clara's plan, and pretend to be
fond of Tom.   I can always alter the plan if I
find that it does not succeed.   I must see what
effect it has on Mr. Merle.

Only, because I love him so much, I shall
always call him Cecil in future in these secret
pages of my diary.   I know that if I let him
see that I loved him he would hate me.   And
if he hated me, I should die.   Clara is quite
right about his boldness, and I feel sure that
with him an obstacle *would* prove an allurement.   If it makes him declare his—ah, I can't
write it!   He is coming to dinner to-morrow
night, and I will write again then.

September 5th.—I have just come up from
the drawing-room.   I talked to Tom most of
dinner-time, and I played the accompaniments
to Tom's songs.   I told him that I should have
" The Devout Lover " ringing in my head all
night.   Afterward I talked to Cecil—chiefly
about Tom's prospects at Cambridge.   I watched
most anxiously to see what effect this had on
Cecil.   I could not discover that it had any

effect at all; he does not let one see very easily what his feelings are. He ought to, I think. Tom, however, was very much elated; I thought he would never let go of my hand when he said good-night. This is unfortunate, but I must go on with the plan a little longer, until I see things more clearly.

When one sees the two men together, one cannot help noticing Cecil's distinct superiority. He is really god-like, far beyond all other men. Charles Leader appealed to me to some extent; my friendship for him was invested with a certain sentiment. I was a simple country girl, and I was misled at the time by my feelings. When Tom came, he appealed to me far more, but although I have always tried to be kind to him, I can see now that I never loved him. Cecil, on the other hand, does not exactly appeal to me; he masters me, absorbs me. To see him is joy unspeakable; to think of him is the rapture that almost tortures. How utterly I love him!

Something within me seems to tell me that Clara was right. Cecil is so brilliant, so bold, so intensely masculine, that the thought of a rival would add to the ardor of his love; I feel that I know his nature perfectly; he is made to conquer, and he would care nothing for a victory which involved no fighting. Yes, for one day more I will carry on the plan, and then I will

let him say what he will be dying to say. I
hope it will be in the conservatory. It seems so
nice to think of it happening in a dim light,
among the flowers, and ferns, and things.

September 7th.—It does cut me to the heart to
be so cruel to Cecil, and it hurts me ever so much
more to be so kind to Tom. But this at any rate
will be the last day of it. I have given the plan
every chance now, and I do not mean to conceal
my real feelings so completely for the future.

Mr. Merle came for tennis this afternoon. I
made papa take him off to see our collection of
early prayer-books. When he came back I had
managed to get rid of Aunt Mary, and was
seated in the summer-house alone with Tom. I
was distinctly cold in my manner to Cecil, and
tried to make him feel *de trop.* I thought he
would be very furious; but he was not. He was
very polite, and seemed to be very careful what
he was saying. He left early. I must get
ready for dinner, and have no time to write any
more now, but I shall add a word or two perhaps
when I come up to bed.

10.30.—It is all over! Let me set down as
calmly as my despair will allow me how everything happened.

After dinner Tom suggested that I should go
out with him into the garden, as it was cool
and pleasant there. I thought this would be
a good opportunity to begin to let him down

easily; so I went with him. But I could not let him down, because he hardly spoke; he seemed strange in his manner, I thought. We wandered into the conservatory, where it was almost dark; and then quite suddenly he put his arm round my waist, and—*kissed me.* I die with shame! How can men be such brutes —such gross, coarse, unmannerly brutes! I told him that I hated him; he wanted to excuse himself, but I would not listen, and hurried back into the drawing-room.

Papa was standing on the hearth-rug with an open letter in his hand, which he had been reading to Aunt Mary. She looked at me rather curiously. The letter was from Cecil—no, Mr. Merle; for I must call him Cecil no longer— and apologized for not coming to sav good-by. He has been suddenly called away, and is going abroad, probably for two years.

Oh, my heart is broken, and I would that my life might end to-night!

4—From the "Daily Telegraph" of Sept. 7th
(A Year Later)

Leader—Marshe.—On the 4th inst., at St. Margaret's, Carleston, by the Rev. Patrick Downs, Charles, eldest son of the late Charles Leader, of Tredennick, Cornwall, to Millicent, only daughter of the late Rev. Hubert Marshe, formerly rector of Carleston.

IV

CONCEALED ART

(EXTRACT FROM THE DIARY OF EDWARD TINNERSLEY)

March 21st.—Dined to-night with the Merricks. There were a lot of people there. The Birnleys looked as profuse as ever. Old Dr. Farnham told the story of the blind zebra once more. Eric Thorn bored me. And I forgave them all, because I was too pleased with myself to bear enmity to anybody—in a word, I do believe that I am at last making some progress with Maud. I blundered before, because I did not quite understand her. And now I believe that I know her better than she knows herself; and consequently I can play my cards—I can create the right impression.

Maud Merrick, my tall, noble beauty, you would be very angry if you could read this. You are affectionate, but you use always a decent reserve. You would not care to know that anybody had seen through the veil, and knew all your little likes and dislikes, all your personal qualities, and even the one or two infirmities of your character. I know them all, my dear Maud, and I do not mind telling you in the pages of my diary—that you want too much. Your ideal man, the man you are looking for, the man you mean to marry, does not exist, and never did exist except in books. You want, in the man of your choice, intellect, courage, strength, physique, chivalry, and purity. · You do not care for either birth or wealth. We none of us care for birth really, and we all pretend to; we all care very much for wealth, and all pretend not to. (*Mem.*—Work this into epigrammatic form, and use it.) But you are quite genuine about it; you really do not care for either. And yet, on the whole, you ask too much. Take myself, for instance. I can give you intellect, but I must draw my pen through the remainder of your list of requirements. What does it matter? Having intellect, I can make you believe that I have all, or nearly all, the rest. Maud Merrick, you are clever in your way, but I am cleverer, and I gain some advantage from having absolutely no scruples. You may throw down your cards. The game is won, and I have won it.

Physique? Well, I must let that pass. I have not the beefy good looks of Eric Thorn. No amount of intellect can make a five-foot-six man, bent with the sedentary profession of authorship, into a straight young giant like Thorn.

There he has the advantage of me, and he may make the most of it. I am not fool enough to sneer at his good points to her. I gaze admiringly at him, playing tennis at a little distance, and say to her, "What a splendid fellow Eric is! It is a positive pleasure to look at him. Ah! I'd give all I have in the world to——" and then I stop short. I do not sigh, because that would be unmanly, and would seem to make too much of it. I look rather sad, and then cheer up suddenly, as if with a slight effort, and talk brightly to her about something impersonal. A girl I knew once told me that she rather liked me when I looked sad, but that when I laughed, or when I was angry, my face was positively hideous. I think she was right.

My dear Maud, I did all this, and I was charmed to find that the little trick made every point that I intended. You noted my generosity to a rival, and associated it in your mind with chivalry; you noted my humility; you noted that I lingered on so personal a subject as my own appearance only for the second when my enthusiastic admiration of Eric reminded me of it, and that I turned back at once to the decent reserve which is a sign of strength, and which you yourself maintain so well; you noted my sadness and sympathized. That was why you said a pretty thing to me about my book, "A Froward Woman," soon afterward. You wish to console me; if you console me now, you will love me soon.

Courage? I have not got a particle of it. Men of delicate taste, of the subtle, critical faculty, of poetical imagination, are often cowards. I am a coward, and I make you believe, Maud, that I am brave. How? Chiefly by telling you that I am a coward. It is just a little amusing that it should be so, but it is.

"I hate going over Putney Bridge at night. I am always afraid that some poor wretch will jump into the water, and that I shall not dare to jump off the bridge after him."

You replied just as I knew I should make you reply. "You would do it, though, because you think you wouldn't. No coward ever dares to confess cowardice."

You were a little pleased at your own insight into human nature, and you believed what you said. You are one of those women who like to go a little deep; but I always know precisely how deep you will go, and I go a little deeper.

Chivalry and purity? Ah, Maud, I need say nothing; you will believe the best, because you have no reason to think otherwise. You do not know the story of that girl I knew once, who said she rather liked me when I looked sad. I will take care you never know it. Though I am writing in cipher and in a diary which is always kept under lock and key, I do not care

5

to put down that story. I have no scruples; I
do things; but I sometimes hate myself for a
little while when I think about them afterward.

I got on very well with Maud to-night. Her
father and Lady Merrick both like me, I think.
The dinner itself was capital, and I was in a
good talking mood. But I am getting into the
habit of bringing out my impromptus a little
too quickly. A slight pause makes them look
more natural; if the pause is too long they seem
labored and not really impromptu. It is not an
easy thing to get quite right; I must practise
it. When one dines with the Merricks, I find
that one has to be kind to the Birnleys. That
is a little hard on me, because I hate the *nouveau riche*, and also because I have some particularly smart things ready to say about the
Birnleys. However, Maud will have it so.
She says that they are awfully good-hearted
people, and not really vulgar, but only a little
ignorant, and that they are sensitive and quick
to see when a jest is aimed at them. (*Mem.*—
Work off the smart things in a sketch of the
nouveau riche. Found it on the Birnleys and
describe their country-house. Tell the story of
how Birnley shot the keeper.) Maud sang one
song to-night—some Italian thing, I don't know
the name. She has a fine contralto.

I walked back with Thorn, and we talked
about old college days together. That man is

a damnable nuisance. In speaking of college days to Maud, I must either tell the plain truth or run the risk that she will find me out from Thorn. And I can't use any of my old good things in talking to her, because she might quote them to Thorn, and he has heard them all before. How the brute would jeer at me for the repetition!

My diary, I think I should go mad without you. It rests me to write in your pages without effort. I need not mind being dull here. In my talk and my books I have to maintain a reputation. Here I can be dull and I can tell the truth. I feel to-night like a tired actor, glad to get into his dressing-room and be rid of his wig and make-up. (*Mem.*—Might elaborate that sentence a little, and then use it.) I will not write any more now. I am going to bed. I ought to do some work first, but I cannot. My brain is full of madness and Maud. If I am to get any sleep, I must go back to the old remedy. But I will never use it again after to-night.

March 30th.—I have just finished my sketch of the Birnleys, and I really do not think I ever did anything better in my life. I stopped at their place for a month last year, and I flatter myself that I have got the people, the house, and the furniture, with the accuracy of a photograph. I've just touched it up a little in places,

but that is all.   I've made Mrs. Birnley a shade
more vulgar, perhaps, than she really is.   I
shall call it "The Barnsley Menagerie."   I shall
not put my initials to it, because that would
ruin me with Maud, and would also stop the
Birnleys from inviting me this year.   I shall
send it to *The Drop Scene* because none of them
know that I write for that paper.   Eric Thorn
had a story in it last week—sporting and stupid,
like its author.   That man would make a very
good navvy.   What ails him that he should be
called to the bar and dabble in literature?

April 3d.—Eric Thorn has just been here.
He has proposed to Maud Merrick, and has been
refused.   I *am* glad.

"We're old friends," he said to me, "and I
thought I would tell you all about it.   No one
can read your book, 'A Froward Woman,' and
doubt your sympathy, old man."

I assured him that I was sorry for him, deeply
sorry.

"Yes, Ted," he replied, "I know it.   I thought
once that I had a chance.   She seemed to like
me once, and then she found out that I knew
the author of 'A Froward Woman,' and asked
me—or made Lady Merrick ask me—to bring
you there.   Well, the natural consequences
have followed.   I can't talk as you can.   You're
always sparkling and amusing.   And you're a
better fellow."

I said something deprecatory here, but he went on.

"No, Ted, I am quite right. Do you know what she said to me before she ever met you? She said that she thought the author of 'A Froward Woman' must have a noble nature. I reminded her of that the other day, and asked her if she thought she was right. 'I know I was right,' she replied. It was the nearest thing to a confidence I ever had from her. You always depreciate yourself when you are talking, but you sometimes let a little thing drop by accident, or do not quite succeed in hiding it. I've noticed those little things, and they are all evidence that Maud was right. You may sneer at yourself as much as you please, but you don't deceive me. You have a noble nature, nobler than mine. Besides, you are my intellectual superior. Look at your fame in the world. I have written a lot of things, and I've only got one story printed. It was in *The Drop Scene*. Did you see the note about it in *The London Review* this week—cutting it all to bits?"

I said that I had not seen the note. I wrote it, by the way. I also asked him what his point was in accusing me of being noble and intellectual.

"Because your absurd humility has made you blind. Let me ask you one question—

we are old friends. Do you like Maud Merrick?"

"I love her with all my soul," I said solemnly, seeing what was coming.

"And you never told her, because you knew that I loved her too, and because you wanted to give me the first chance."

I assumed an unnatural manner, and intentionally spoke a little more quickly than usual. "No, no—not at all—you're quite mistaken. I only waited to be quite sure that she loved me, and I never thought you would speak so soon. On my word, I would have done you a bad turn with her, if I could." What a curious thing human nature is! Every word of this was true, and yet he didn't believe it. I had an impression that he wouldn't believe it.

"My dear fellow," said Thorn, "why try to hide your generosity by talking such absolute nonsense? She herself told me that you were always singing my praises to her."

My dear simpleton, didn't you know that it is quite possible to ruin a man's chances with a woman by praising him very carefully? I praised you, my dear Thorn, with the utmost discretion. He continued:

"In this point I am going to try not to be less generous than you. I feel sure that Maud Merrick loves you. I suspected it even before I spoke to her, and I only spoke because I could not bear the suspense any longer. It may seem strange that I—a rejected lover—should come to tell you this, but I felt that I owed it to you; besides, I want her to be happy. You are the only man in the world who can make her happy."

I thanked him. "And you?" I asked.

"I'm going away, Ted, going to travel and forget it. I start on the 8th. I will see you again before I go."

He went soon after this. He looks terribly knocked over. All this is going splendidly. Now I have three things before me—a letter to write to Sir Charles Merrick, two-thirds of a bottle of very excellent brandy, and the proofs of "The Barnsley Menagerie" to correct. I will take them in that order.

April 5th.—Maud, my beautiful Maud, has promised to be my wife.

April 6th.—A most terrible thing has happened. *The Drop Scene* has been sent me here with my article "The Barnsley Menagerie" in it, *signed with my initials.*

How on earth did they get there? I must have added them from force of habit when I corrected the proof. I remember that it was late on the night of the 3d that I corrected it. It was the night I wrote to her father, and then I——ah, yes, I remember now.

As far as I can see, there is nothing to do but

to calculate what will happen, and then see how it can be stopped. In the first place, the Birnleys will read the article; they will certainly see that it is meant for them, and that it must have been written by some one who stayed at their place in the country; they know that I write for the press and they will see my initials. I fancy that they will all go mad. They will call me hard names and will cut me dead forever and ever. Well, I care nothing about the Birnleys. They may go to the devil.

But Maud—my beautiful, noble Maud—what will she think? Now I come to think of it, she will have a little piece of evidence that the Birnleys will not have, and which will make her doubly sure that I am the author of that article. It commences with a little epigram of mine on birth and wealth. Now, on the day after I wrote the article, I called at their house with Eric Thorn. In the course of conversation I dropped that very epigram. She heard it and noticed it. I had meant to strike it out when I got my article in proof, but I suppose I forgot it. I cannot have been quite myself that night. She will simply hate me and despise me. I can imagine her eyes flashing, and the tender sympathy she will show with her good-hearted Birnleys. It would be pretty to watch, if one could be a little more outside it. However, I do not fancy it is quite checkmate. I will have a quiet pipe, think out a probable story to account for everything, and go to bed. I am sure my doctor would recommend me a little chloral to-night, considering the excited state of my nerves. What a letter I shall get to-morrow morning!

April 7th (morning).—Here is the letter. I see by the date that it was written yesterday:

"SIR:—I read this morning your article in *The Drop Scene*, entitled 'The Barnsley Menagerie.' Kindly consider my engagement to you at an end. If you wish for a more definite reason, I may say that the article must have been written by an insufferable, vulgar, cruel cad. I know it is yours by the initials, by your acquaintance with the Birnleys, and by the fact that you have used in it an epigram which I. heard from your own lips. On the whole, I am thankful that you have been so stupid as to allow your real character to be seen.

"I saw Mr. and Mrs. Birnley this afternoon. She sat fierce and dry-eyed, reading your spiteful article again and again. She hardly spoke to me. He tried to take it more easily. 'It's partly my own fault,' he said, 'but it is rather hard that we should be treated like this, Maud, by a man who was our guest. We did our best to entertain him when he was here. But still it's partly true—that article. I'm a very good manufacturer, but I only made a fool of myself when I tried to play the country gentleman. And I'm clumsy with a gun—that's true.' He paused a second, and then looked at his wife. 'My God! Maud,' he flashed out suddenly, 'if only I could have the thrashing of the hound who wrote that!' I wish he had. He is an old man, but vigorous. I think he could thrash you well. How could you be so cruel to people who had tried to be kind to you?

"I have no patience to write more. You will oblige me by not answering this letter, or calling at our house, or making any attempt whatever to see me.

"MAUD MERRICK.

"*P. S.*—O Ted, how *could* you do it? I did really love you once, and now I hate you."

Now, that is not altogether a nice letter to receive. "An insufferable, vulgar, cruel cad "—I suppose that is very much what I am, judged by ordinary standards, but I have always had wits enough to hide it so far. It's not my fault. I was born so, and no one could expect me to do anything else but hide the real self. I do not really care, as long as I can keep Maud. I *must* have Maud. I thought of an explanation last night, but it is not absolutely satisfactory. I will go and get something particularly pleasant and inspiring in the shape of lunch. I shall be able to think better after a half-bottle of champagne.

(*Evening.*) Eric Thorn has just been here. Really, he is a most useful person. When he came in, he was as white as death, and there was a queer sort of huskiness in his voice.

"Ted, old man," he said, "I've just been telling lies, any amount of lies."

"All this I steadfastly believe," I replied. He went on talking:

"I called at the Merricks' to-night to say good-by. Sir Charles came into the room with that number of *The Drop Scene* in his hand, open at your article: 'Thorn, old fellow, I want you just to read that.' There was no one else in the room. I sat down and read it. Of course, I saw that it was yours, and that the Merricks would in all probability have nothing more to do with you. Ted, how could you write such a thing about people who were so kind to you?"

This made me a little angry. "Possibly," I said, "I could give a sufficient explanation to any one who had a right to ask for it."

"Well, I didn't see how it could be quite explained away. Yet all the time I was reading it, I thought I could see how it happened. You caricatured the Birnleys, but half unconsciously. Your tremendous power of satire carried you away, and made you say things that you didn't really mean. I know that a man who behaved with the generosity that you showed to me about Maud could not possibly do a shabby thing intentionally. I know how hard it is to criticise one's own work, and I felt sure that you had failed to see how certain it was that the Birnleys would be offended. If you had meant it as an intentional insult, you would not have been fool enough to put your initials to it, and to commence it with an epigram which both Maud and myself had heard from your lips. It was the only slip I ever knew you make, and I felt sure that you would never do that kind of thing again, as soon as you saw the distress that it caused. Well, I knew Maud would give you up, and break your heart over it and her own as well. So I made up my mind on the spur of the moment, and took the liberty of claiming the authorship of the work as my own. Our initials are the same, you know, Ted."

"You did that?" I said. I own that he had surprised me. "How did you make the old man believe it?"

"I pointed out that the initials were mine. that you never wrote for *The Drop Scene*, and that I had a story in it a short time before. I told him that I borrowed the epigram at the commencement of the article from you, that I had stopped with the Birnleys, and that I didn't care for them. I said that I couldn't see much harm in the article, and that *The Drop Scene* liked a thing to have a few personalities in it."

"How did he take it?"

"He was very sad about it. They've known me for a long time, you see. 'I can't think how you came to write it, Thorn,' he said. 'You ought not to have done it. You have caused my daughter and all of us to do a friend of yours a great injustice; and you have given great pain to people whose hospitality you enjoyed. I hate saying it, but I must—you cannot come here any more. It is well that you are leaving the country. Take a word of advice before you go, from an old man who was once glad to have you for his friend—if you can't be smart without being shabby, let it alone —let it alone, my boy!' Then he touched the bell, and I retired ignominiously."

He rose to go, paused a moment, and said: "That's the story I told, and you must back it up. Good-by, old man. I will find a new character for myself abroad somewhere."

He tried to hide it, but I could see that he thought he had acted generously, and naturally that maddened me. I could not allow him to think that he had put me under any obligation. I like to take the conceit out of young men of the type of Eric Thorn. The self-sacrificing saint is too provoking for anything.

"I am very sorry, Thorn," I said, "that you

have destroyed your own character, stolen my
property, and told some most abominable lies,
because it was all unnecessary.   I know you did
it for my sake, but you would have served me
better if you had trusted me more.   How could
you think I should be such a blackguard as to
caricature a host of mine in the public press?"

"You didn't write it, then?" he stammered
out.

"Yes, I wrote it—wrote it for practice to improve me in delineation of character—but not
for publication.   It was published without my
consent and without my knowledge.   Do you
know the editor of *The Drop Scene?*"

"No."

I was delighted to learn this.   "I am very
sorry to hear it," I said, "because, if you had
known him, you would have understood my
explanation better.   He is the most unscrupulous
man engaged on the press, and the finest critic.
I took him my sketch of the Birnleys to look at
and criticise as a literary performance.   He
liked it and wanted to print it.   I told him
that I would not have it printed.   He offered
me a very high price; I replied that the sketch
was from real life, and that there was not
enough money in London to buy it; that I
would sooner have my right hand cut off than
make fun at the expense of a friend and host of
mine.   I took the manuscript away with me

there and then. He must have expected this, for he had had a copy made of it. It was published without my consent. I should certainly have prosecuted."

" And now? "

" Well, now I must leave it."

"It would be possible to explain to the Merricks my innocent deception, and for you to clear yourself by telling them what you have told me. Would not that be best? "

This was a little difficult; for if there had been a single word of truth in my story of the unscrupulous editor, it would have been much the best.

"I think not," I said; "I think not. You have gone too far. Of course, I know that your motive for the story you told Sir Charles Merrick was innocent enough. But I might find it difficult to persuade him of this. As a literary performance, my article has attracted considerable attention! From that point of view it is undoubtedly good. I am afraid that Sir Charles will think that you wanted the literary credit of it, and then backed out to avoid the moral infamy. I do not think your position would in any way be improved."

He looked at me curiously for a second or two. "Good-by, then," he said. "I'm sorry I was so stupid and mistaken." He went out in a dejected, hopeless way. I fancy he has a lurking. suspicion. Let it lurk! He's going away and I shall not be bothered with him any more.

So the Merricks believe now that Eric Thorn wrote that article, do they? I think then that I will answer Maud's letter in spite of her injunctions. I should imagine that my beautiful Maud wishes now that she had never written it. Never mind—I can be magnanimous, Maud, and very high-souled. This is what I shall write to you, Maud:

"DEAR MISS MERRICK:—I am sorry that you could ever have imagined that I wrote 'The Barnsley Menagerie.' Had I done so, you would have been quite just in your criticism of me.

"I can only prove to you that I did not write it by telling you who the real author is, and this I cannot do. He confessed the authorship to me in confidence. Perhaps he may afterward decide to let his name be known. But, if he does not, I cannot tell you—I cannot break my word to him.

> " 'I could not love thee half so much,
> Loved I not honor more.'

"Forgive me for having disobeyed your command by writing this letter. I could not rest until I had made an appeal to you to believe my word for the present, and to trust to time to

prove the truth of it. Believe me, yours in all
sincerity, EDWARD TINNERSLEY."

And this is what I shall write to the editor of
The Drop Scene:

"DEAR TOM:—No end of a row about 'The
Menagerie.' Keep my name dark, for God's
sake, and I'll do you something ripping for next
week. It's rare sport at present; but the country wouldn't hold me if it were known that I
wrote it. Say a man called Eric Thorn wrote
it, if asked. It's safe. Yours ever,
"TED TINNERSLEY."

And now I think I may go to bed with a
clear conscience. I shall be able to sleep all
right to-night. Good-night, my darling Maud.
I am afraid that you will lie awake, thinking
of those hard names you called me.

April 8th.—A very pretty, penitent letter
from Maud. She seems really distressed at
having written to me so fiercely. She has not
an atom of pride or reserve left in her now.
"Eric Thorn has confessed that he wrote the
hateful thing. It was noble of you to keep his
name secret because of your promise to him.
Are men always so loyal to their friends?"

That is really very nice. "Forgive me! forgive me!" she says at the close of the letter.

6

Yes, Maud, I forgive you, and I will call on you to-day to say so. I am feeling particularly magnanimous just now. With what sorrow I shall speak of the shocking behavior of my former friend, Eric Thorn! And how really high-toned I shall be! I really must stop to laugh.

To-night, Maud, you will know the joys of sin forgiven; they are not quite so great as the joys of sins concealed. I have tried both. (*Mem.*—Might put that into the mouth of some cynical blackguard in a story—it's not bad.)

In a few months' time, Maud, you will be mine indeed; and then will come the disillusion. You will know that I really am what you once called me, "a vulgar, cruel cad." I was born so. I tried to be better once, but it was of no use. There is a certain horror about that which comes over me suddenly sometimes. It is an awful thing to be hateful and to know that it is of no use to try to be anything else. In the midst of success, and high spirits, and jeers at everything, that thought suddenly comes over me, and I writhe. I seem to see the devil himself sitting in the room with me, looking at me and smiling horribly. And with him is that other girl of whom I have spoken—she drowned herself. She does not smile. She just sits and scares—no, I won't write any more. (*Mem.*— Some of the above paragraphs might be useful for a sketch of character, called "Remorse.")

Now, gentlemen, your offers. This maiden
    sings and dances,
  She's beautiful, and innocent, and lively as
    the day.
You bid a fortune? Thank you, sir. I'm
    waiting for advances;
  And you a life's devotion? Here, take that
    boy away.
A title? Come, that's better. Now it's going,
    going, going—
  She is but seventeen, sirs, and lovely as you
    see—
Gone! Madam, you're the property, you will
    be pleased at knowing,
  Of a genial old roué of the age of sixty-three.

Now here's a nice cold chicken and a bottle
    from the ice, sirs—
  Ah, you dramatic critics, aren't you hungry?
    Won't you bid?
Won't some one offer me his soul—a very mod-
    erate price, sirs?
  You sold *your* soul last week, sir? Yes—
    dear me—of course you did!

Here's a ticket for a prize-fight.   The magis-
    trate's the winner,
    After some sharp contention—the bidding's
        getting bold.
Here's a poet.   What, no offers?   Won't some
    one bid a dinner?
    Take the brute away and drown him;   he
        never will be sold.

And lastly I would offer here an over-dose of
    chloral.
    That boy again?   Bids twopence?   Why
        don't you turn him out?
I may mention that the notion that suicide's
    immoral
    Is an antiquated fallacy—it's utterly played
        out.
We cannot think of twopence; now, I'm wait-
    ing for advances—
    There's not a death more painless, and I'll
        guarantee it true—
Oh!   Here's a better offer from the maid who
    sings and dances.
    Thank you, maiden—I'd a fancy I should sell
        this lot to you.

V

WHEN THAT SWEET CHILD LAY DEAD

A Vigil

It was quite a little room. The window looked out on a garden, on an orchard beyond it, and on the old quiet hills that had made the child understand what "far away" meant. She had heard, months ago, the bees monotonously, musically busy among the garden flowers; she had watched in the orchard the blossoms delicate with the fragile grace of immaturity, and when the autumn came, she had seen the boughs twisted and bent with their effort to do good, with their burden of fruit; she had strayed through the park-land; she had seen the sun set over the hills, when far up the sky went the touch of pale gold on clouds that were like angels' wings. Her eyes had grown brighter, always, and her thoughts stranger as she watched; it had made her, the child of a musician, want to hear the music that in her serious moments had seemed to understand her best. She was not to see such things, nor hear them, nor understand any more. On this eve of the

New Year she lay motionless, arranged with
white hands crossed, on the bed in one corner
of the room; the trees in the orchard were gaunt
and black, mocked by cruel winds; the snow
drove and drove; the year's last day died out in
darkness.

Everything in the little room—a little room
in a great house—was very neat and orderly.
Some one had taken away from the low table
by the bedside the row of medicine bottles—
grim reminders of futile effort—and had placed
there an old blue-and-white bowl, full of Christmas roses. In the fireplace the logs burned
brightly. She did not need the grace of the
flowers nor the warmth of the fire any more.
But some one had seen to these things—had
done them from a sentiment; nearly all the best
things that one does are done from a sentiment.
Flowers and fire were useless; but when that
sweet child lay dead, to those in the great house
all things had seemed useless. She had been
very dear to all of them; they thought her
lovelier, brighter, gentler than other children.
Yet her chief charm was, perhaps, that she had
returned their affection; she had loved people
very easily—even unlikely people. Downstairs
the servants who had waited on her were ludi-
crously pathetic; it was a chance whether one
who had seen them would have laughed or felt
like weeping. Two maids, who had known

enmity from some jealousy about that child, now snuffled together in common sorrow, grotesquely genuine. "And Mr. Richards feels it too," said one of them, "though it's little as Mr. Richards ever shows." Richards was the old butler, a stern man, made cynical possibly by too intimate a knowledge of the wine trade. He was in his pantry, polishing silver very briskly, almost jauntily; he caught sight of her cup, a christening gift; he recalled how she had once wrung from his sternness some slight concession about a new footman, really by no means up to his work; he began at once to whistle the gayest of tunes in a desperate whispered whistle, then stopped suddenly, made an involuntary curious sound in his throat, and went on polishing furiously. Later on his manner grew icy.

From her room one could now have heard very faintly the sound of the organ being played in the wide gallery which ran from wing to wing of the house. It was her father, the great composer, who was playing. She had been his only child, and her mother had died in her babyhood. So he was alone now. He had been saying that to himself during the day: "I am quite alone now." There were other people in the house, relations more or less near; but, as far as his sorrow was concerned, they were a hundred miles away. He had been happy, as

some count happiness; he had loved his art and
had been great in it; he had wealth, and could
follow art for art's sake. Only he was human.
and had not escaped human joys; nor the sorrows that follow them so closely; he had loved
a wife and child, and he had lost them. That
afternoon he had sat quite alone in his studio,
thinking. A salver, laden with letters, was
brought into the room. He opened a few of
the letters. They were all well-meaning, and
yet so futile. He felt that he could read no
more of them, and that he could not keep quiet
and inactive any longer. He went up into the
long gallery and paced up and down. Then he
arranged the mechanism which blew the organ,
and opened the instrument, and lit the candles
on either side of it. The rest of the gallery lay
in darkness. And then he sat down to play.
The music was sorrow without consolation;
religion without hope.

In the little room the flicker of fire-light fell
on the golden hair and delicate upturned face of
that sweet child. Did it matter to the rest of
the world—to things that are inarticulate, or
even voiceless, and, as some think, inanimate?
Were the flowers that she had loved sorry, or
the winds that had played in her hair? Perhaps on that bleak eve of the New Year there
was something said that one would not have
heard as one hears a voice, which might through

a dream have won its way to words. What did the Christmas roses think about it in that old blue-and-white bowl on the table by her side? Was it all nothing to them when that sweet child lay dead?

. . . .

It was sheer carelessness, of course, and had not been done with any evil intention at all. But that did not alter the facts of the case—his stem was not in the water, and he had felt a little wilted at the very outset.

Flowers choose their own names, and this one had called himself Wilkinson. He had seen the name on a scrap of newspaper that had been blown down the garden walk, and never ought to have been there, and was the under-gardener's fault. Wilkinson knew that owing to sheer carelessness his death would be hastened by some few hours; he did not mind the death (flowers, possibly from vanity, love to be cut and put in vases; and it is heaven to them to be worn in a girl's hair), but he did object to anything like carelessness. He liked people to do their whole duty. Even while selecting the name of Wilkinson he had deprecated the untidiness of the under-gardener.

"Cut me and put me in a bowl, if you like," he remarked snappishly. "If you think me beautiful, you couldn't do any better. Only *do* it. Don't half do it. Don't leave me with my stem out of the water in this sickening way. If you do, you commit sin; and I can't bear to see it done." He was not addressing any of the other flowers in particular, he was merely soliloquizing on the subject of strict duty, which was an unpleasing habit that he had. No flowers care in the least about death, except the sweet violets, who have some mysterious love secrets of their own, never properly understood, which they do not like to be interrupted. Few flowers are quite so strict or quite so sharp-tempered as Wilkinson was.

"It wasn't *her* fault," pleaded a little bud, called Candor, who had been looking at the sweet child motionless on her bed.

"My dear child," said Wilkinson, rather patronizingly, "how very young you are! Any one could tell you were a bud. Don't you know that sweet child's dead? She's no use—can't put flowers in water any more—so they'll throw her away. They ought to have thrown her away before, I should have thought; but human beings are always so careless and untidy."

"She's very pretty," said Candor; "very pretty indeed. I wish they had put me in her hair. Who was it placed us in this bowl?"

"Ah! yes. You were too young to remember it. It was Richards who put us here—and left my stem out of the water. How *mad* such thoughtlessness does make me! You're too

young to be worn in a girl's hair. But Richards
might perhaps have selected something—something a little more full blown. I don't refer to
myself in particular, of course, although for the
matter of that, as far as mature beauty is concerned—well, well, it's not for me to say."

"Death is very beautiful. Do human beings
like to die?"

Wilkinson shrugged his petals impatiently.
"What a perfectly bud-like remark! Death is
not beautiful. Death is nothing. You simply
stop, that's all. As you are generally feeling
rather faded, you're not sorry to stop. But
you're not particularly glad. It's pleasanter, of
course, to die in a girl's hair than to live in a
garden, especially where the under-gardener's
so grossly untidy. I believe you have been
talking to those violets," he added, rather
sharply.

"No, really, I haven't. Why did you ask
that?"

"They've got some sentimental ideas about
death. No, I don't suppose human beings mind
it. I don't see how they can mind a thing
which is of absolutely no importance."

"They live longer than we do."

"They live an unconscionable time, most of
them, especially under-gardeners. That is probably because they have not our advantages,
and do not understand. That child has stopped

rather early—yes, she is a sweet child. I can remember when I was quite a bud, she went past laughing. You should have seen the sunlight on her hair!"

There was a long pause. Candor spoke at last:

"Wilkinson, do you think anything *really* stops, or is it just seeming? She is so pretty, and you remember her laughter, and any flower would have been glad to die in that beautiful hair. It can't have all been to no purpose."

Wilkinson was distressed—deeply distressed. "You pain and grieve me more than I can say. The old faiths are all going. Have you not been taught to believe in the nothingness of everything? Why do you listen to the hideous voice of emotion?"

Candor grew almost passionate. "I *must*. If I did not listen I should not know what to do for sorrow! She is lovely. She is an angel's dream—not dead, but come true at last. Sweet child, speak to me and tell me that I am right. Speak only once and tell me this trifling—this life and death—is not everything. Tell me that there is more beyond—beyond."

"You are sickly and heterodox," said Wilkinson sternly. "There is nothing beyond. I believe—nay, I know—that death is entire cessation. And I am going to drop."

He dropped fragmentarily. It is ordained

that in its last moments even the tidiest flower
shall be untidy.   And Candor still waited; but
all was silent in that little room.

.   .   .   .

Now, the winds are spirits, lost spirits; they
never rest, and they ever long for rest.

That night a great wind swept past the house,
ice-cold and howling with misery.   It beat on
the windows of that little room until they
shook; and then it went flying onward through
the driving snow.   After it came another, softly
pattering, like the pattering of a child's feet as it
shuffles through the crisp, fallen leaves.   These
two winds were spirits, without shape to human
eyes; and yet a dreamer—a musician, perhaps,
seated at the organ, alone with sorrow—might
have imagined something.   He might have
seen them—the first like a gaunt woman, with
flying robes and hair; the second like a girl-
child, with an old man's malice and a devil's
cruelty in her look, and to the dreamer their
voices might have grown articulate.

"Perdita," said the young wind, as side by
side they sped onward into the night, "did you
not see as we went past the house?   In one of
the rooms a child is lying; a beautiful child,
and she is dead; I shook the window to frighten
her, but she never moved.   Can I not do anything to hurt her?   I hate all beautiful things."

"No, we can do nothing, Ira.   I, too, used

to hate as you hate, but with me it has worn
itself out. I am tired, and cold, and miserable.
But there is no rest—no rest anywhere. We
can do nothing to hurt that child and nothing
to help her. She is dead."

"I would help no one, but I would hurt her.
Can we not reach her, even though she be dead?
What is death?"

Perdita seemed now to be speaking to herself
rather than Ira. "It was a thousand years ago
that they sent me here—they to whom a thousand
years are but as a day. Beyond this world, beyond the tangle of which this world is a thread,
I lived in broader space, in brighter light, in
warmer, clearer air. I do not remember what
it was that I did, but for my punishment they
sent me here to roam forever up and down. For
a thousand years I have never rested; I have
seen the children of men grow up, and fall, and
die; and I have found out many secrets; but I
do not yet know what death is."

"I too," said Ira, "came from that place of
which you speak. With me it was but a day
ago; yet I, too, cannot remember what it was
that I did. But I have been punished—punished
until there is nothing left in me but hatred. I
long to wreck the ships and tear down the
trees. Nothing will make me happy any more,
and I am most miserable when I destroy. Yet
I cannot help longing to destroy."

"It does not matter," Perdita answered. "The longing will wear itself out. You may grow gentle and play with the flowers. That will not matter either. You will always be unhappy and you will never rest. Oh, if one could rest! If one could be still for a little while, only a little while!"

"In that great house the child that was dead was still—motionless. What is death?"

There was a pause—a long pause before the voice of Perdita spoke in reply:

"Can it be? Can it be that we are already dead? Can it be that the punishment of which we spoke was nothing else but death, and that death means the torture of endless unrest? Perhaps the spirit of that child is out in this lonely night, suffering as we suffer."

"I feared that you would say it," whispered Ira. "It is quite true. This night that child is with us. Did I want to hurt her? That was foolish of me." And Ira laughed savagely.

The two winds sped on together, past an iron coast, over a dark, desolate sea, and on and on. In the long gallery of the house the music was changed; into its sorrow had entered that tragic anger which knows its own impotence.

. . . .

The night had grown very quiet. The furious winds had passed; the sky had cleared. Over the wide lands lay the fallen snow. The child's father had risen from the organ and opened one of the windows. He stood there looking out. Perhaps it was because he thought of the gentleness of falling snow, or because its wonderful whiteness seemed almost like a conscious kindness; but as he looked out into the tranquil night his anger ceased. Far off he heard the flooded river sweep the base of the bridge, and the monotonous sound seemed to him like a consolation, like a consoling voice:

"I am glad because I draw near to the sea. /I shall die, but I shall not be really lost. It is only change. I give myself to the sea, and in return I enter into its strength. The life of a man is but the bandage that blinds his eyes; and he shall never see the great secret until he himself is part of it. All the rivers run into the sea, and all the lives run into the life eternal. No gain is greater than that loss of self."

His own thoughts followed the voice of the river. Could it be that our identity, which we valued so much, was better lost? He had no patience to think the thing out, but he liked that idea of all the lives flowing into the life eternal. He found himself believing in the river's guess-work; or else he had grown tranquil under the tranquillity of the night; or else, perhaps, this quietness was but reaction following upon action, and the bitterness of sorrow had exhausted itself. He cared very little what the reason might be.   He only knew that he was in some wonderful way consoled.   Death was not annihilation.   Death was not punishment.   Death was just the loss of individuality and the gain of something far greater; something which possibly the saints thought when they spoke of perfect communion and of peace that cannot be understood.

He turned instinctively to symbolism and analogy.   That thing for which lovers long— that total surrender of self to the beloved, which love ever desires and ever misses, is the gift that death has for us.   By death we merge into that fulfilment which is past words.

And past music?

He turned once more to the organ—to that mysterious language that can be translated into no known tongue.

"And," said Richards, next morning, "as I stood at the fur end, he began to play.   You won't believe me, Mrs. Smith, and I can't hardly believe myself, but it was one of the 'appiest toons I ever heard him play—regular light. Well, thinks I to myself, this is queer; and there, all of a sudden-like, 'e drops 'is 'ands and bends 'is 'ead low—this way—and begins sobbing—great, gaspin' sobs.   I couldn't bear it.   I come away.   It was too awful!"

7

VI

THE MAGIC MORNING

THE sunlight fell with steady brightness through the haze of a hot morning. A breath of wind came across the heath, over the dusty road, and down the strip of scented garden that lay in front of the white cottage. It lingered for a moment over some very dark wall-flowers, and then passed through the open window into the lower room on the left of the porch, to see what Mervyn Vallend and his young wife Joyce were going to have for breakfast. The pale yellow curtains moved into soft folds as the wind passed; there was no one in the room. It was Sunday, and breakfast was not till nine o'clock. The little silver clock—it had been a wedding present, and looked it—showed that it still wanted a few minutes to nine. The break-fast-table seemed appealing and rather solitary; it was quite ready. Everything on it was fresh and spotless. There were a handful of loosely-made white roses in a low glass bowl in the centre; the shaft of mote-speckled light touched the bright silver and a crimson fragrant heap of strawberries. They lay on their green leaves, and hoped that Joyce would like them when she came downstairs. It was a pretty room, and everything in it seemed very much as it should be.

Joyce loved the extra hour of rest on Sunday mornings. On week-days breakfast was inclined to be rather a hurried affair, because Mervyn had to catch the train which took him up to the city, and Joyce never felt properly awake at eight o'clock. The extra hour made all the difference. Just at present she was gazing meditatively into the looking-glass. She had a sweet, delicate face, gray eyes, and soft fair hair. She was trying to remember the dream she had had during the night; and only had an indistinct idea that it had been a very happy dream. She had been still asleep when Mervyn got up to go down to the river for a swim before breakfast. As she turned from the looking-glass she saw through the window across the heath; Mervyn was coming back along the narrow track that wound through the golden broom and brambles with wet glistening leaves. Joyce turned again to the looking-glass for a second, made some imperceptible feminine alteration, and then ran lightly downstairs, and stood in the porch waiting for him. She had a slight tremble at her heart; and a reason for it. She had only been married two years, and yet last night she had nearly hated Mervyn. She did not hate him now.

He came slowly and easily over the heath. He was wearing flannels. His towel was flung over his shoulder. His cap was pushed at the back of his untidy brown hair. His face was thin and sunburnt. He was tall and straight, and looked younger than he really was. He, too, was wondering at the change this magic morning had made in him. For last night he had thought, almost with despair, that he should never love Joyce any more.

Yet nothing unusual had happened to bring about the sad state of things which had existed on the Saturday. Had anything unusual happened, all might have been well; for they had the sensitive temperament which is irritated by the persistently ordinary and is attracted by the unusual. They had both of them, from the very first, been rather too much inclined to think that things would be different with them than with other people. They had expected love's ecstasy to last; to be always together, and apart from the rest of the world; to live in a continuous exaltation of spirit; to have a perpetual summer—gentle, cultured, and idyllic—in the white cottage, away from the dirt and din of the city. In a word, they had quite forgotten about action and reaction; they had been a little too self-conscious. They were not prigs;

Mervyn was too masculine and Joyce was too feminine for that; besides, an absence of conceit and the presence of a sense of humor saved both of them from being prigs. But in the ecstasy of their love for each other a little of their common sense had evaporated. Even the arrangement of the furniture in the white cottage was rather sentimental.

And the ecstasy had not lasted. It never lasts. So surely as you go upward from one side of the hill, you must, when you have reached the summit, go downward on the other. There are those who have grown bitter about this necessity. And yet it is sometimes very pleasant and quiet in the valley. Mervyn and Joyce had not quite got down into the valley yet, and were feeling rather lost. For a few months after their marriage, Mervyn had gone on making fresh and exquisite discoveries in Joyce's nature; chance words of hers, little gestures, her choice of flowers and music, seemed to illuminate the reason why she was so lovable. Then he reached the point when there seemed to be no more discoveries to make. She was like a beautiful prayer or poem that has been learned by heart and has been said so often that it has lost its meaning. And there were besides a few disillusions. She was too human to be quite perfect. Just that turn of her temperament which made her love the fanciful stories

and verses that Mervyn wrote from time to
time also made her a little unpractical. Sometimes she forgot how much the most spiritual
happiness depends on the most material things.
At first, Mervyn had thought nothing of occa-
sional discomfort; but there came a time when
he noticed it. Joyce was delicate; it was for
this reason that Mervyn had taken the white
cottage; and sometimes, when he got back from
the city, Joyce was too tired to take much notice
of him—to sing to him or talk to him. Then
he would reproach himself for not being able to
take more care of her, for not being able to give
her a more easeful and luxurious life, for not
having waited until he had secured a better
position before he married her. For Mervyn
was not mad enough to think that he could live
by writing fanciful verses; they only were one
of his pleasures; as far as business was concerned, he was the least possible partner in his
father's unromantic firm. He would be a fairly
rich man one day; but at present he was poor
enough to find himself frequently irritated by
limitations. Sometimes the thought had passed
through him swiftly, and the night before it
had not passed, but had lingered on and on—
perhaps it would have been better if he had
not married Joyce; Joyce was not fitted to be
the wife of a poor man. Last night he had
feared that his love for her was slowly wearing

itself out. She, too, had been through similar experiences; she had begun to think that she was losing his sympathy; she did little things on purpose to please him, and he never noticed them. Besides, it was rather lonely in the white cottage when Mervyn was away in the city; and she hated the work of housekeeping, though she did it as faithfully as she could. And there were small worries which tried her and made her fear that she was losing her sweet temper. She had cried herself to sleep on Saturday night, being filled with the idea that Mervyn would have been much happier if he had married a capital housemaid.

They had not openly quarrelled. On the Saturday afternoon Mervyn got back from the city rather earlier than he had expected; he was hot and irritated by some petty business worries. He found the white cottage rather dishevelled. An unclean charwoman was defiling the staircase with her presence. Joyce had been doing accounts; and the accounts were all wrong; and her fingers were all inky. She had a headache, and was depressed, and not inclined to make very much of Mervyn. He walked to the looking-glass and found that he had a smut on his nose. It had probably been there all the hateful morning. He swore gently under his breath; Joyce heard him and looked hurt. He repented, and asked her to come out.

She reminded him that she had the accounts to
do. He told her, rather self-righteously, that
she should have got the accounts done before.
She, looking as if she were being burned at the
stake, but was determined not to mind it, replied that she had a headache. One knows
how such conversations end. Saturday evening
was passed almost in silence. It was all childish enough, but troubles do not have to be
rational to be troublesome. And these childish
troubles had started in both of them a most per-
nicious train of thought, ending in the entirely
unfounded belief that they were not suited for
each other, and did not love each other. But
now all these troubles were yesterday's delu-
sions; they could not stand before this magic
morning.

Mervyn had paused a second just before leaving the bedroom to go down to the river, and
had turned back to look at his sleeping wife.
There was a look on her face that he had never
seen there before; it was a look to win love and
reverence; it was the dignity of a sleeping Ma-
donna. He took off his cap and, bending over
her, kissed her on the forehead—gently so as
not to wake her. Then he went downstairs, and
out through the porch, and up the narrow strip
of garden. Yes, the weather was glorious; but
mere weather was not enough to account for

the splendid exhilaration that filled him. He felt that he liked everything immensely. He watched the bees busy at the work that had been given them; he caught the fragrance of the dark wall-flowers; he heard the repeated calls of the birds—the clear tremble, rise and fall of their music. It was all old; it had all been so before; yet now there was a new wonder in it. There was a new delight in the refreshing plunge into the cold river, and the long, steady swim up against the stream. He was still thinking of this as he came back across the heath. He seemed to have an excess of strength and spirit, a fresh power of enjoyment. As he entered the garden he looked up and saw Joyce—a sweet, graceful figure in gray and white—standing in the porch. There was a light in her eyes which showed him that she too had felt the magic of the morning. Both knew that there was sympathy again between them. She gave him both hands, and he kissed her; it was the kiss of a glad lover—not the perfunctory, matrimonial kiss.

As they sat down to breakfast, both of them could hardly help laughing; they were so pleased at nothing. They refrained, however, owing to the notion—for which something might have been said—that such conduct would be slightly idiotic. Mervyn removed a cover:

"That," he said, "is routine—sheer routine."
"No, no," said Joyce, "it's only poached eggs
—nothing worse, I assure you."
"I meant the number, Joyce.   Don't you see
—the mystic number three?   Anna Martha has
absolutely no variableness, and she won't allow
for it in other people.   She knows that I generally eat two and you generally eat one.   So
she expects us always to do that, and always
sends us just exactly three.   She's cast a sort
of spell over me, and I find myself eating two
eggs when I only want one, simply to satisfy
the passion for regularity in Anna Martha.   I'm
not going to stand it any longer.   To-day I will
only eat one and you shall eat two; and that
will break Anna Martha's clockwork heart."
"But I don't see how she's to know, unless
you tell her, which of us had two."
"That's true, Joyce, horribly true, and I certainly daren't tell her.   Well, I must get out of
the groove, somehow.   I might do it by not
eating any at all, only I happen to be distinctly
hungry," he added, as he helped himself.
They did not always talk such utter nonsense
as this; for both Joyce and Mervyn had as much
intellect as the average man—and perhaps
keener appreciation.   But this morning they
were talking nonsense with a set purpose; and
yet neither of them had any notion that they
were talking with a set purpose at all.   This

happens rather more frequently than is generally supposed. Underneath the words of both of them lay—quite unconsciously—this thought: "We must not let our minds dwell for a moment on yesterday; what took place then was all a mistake, and too horrible to think about; we must forget it, and show that we have forgotten it by being cheerful."

"I've got a new dress on to-day," said Joyce, presently. "Do you like it?"

"Yes; I had been adoring in silence. It really is a lovable sort of a clothing." He paused for a second. "Talking of new things," he added, "when I was going down to the river this morning, I stopped for a second to look at you, and, really, there was something—something indescribable—in your face that I had never seen there before."

Joyce's gray eyes opened a little wider. "How? What do you mean? How did I look?"

"Different."

"Improved—better?"

"Happier—a saintly sort of happiness."

"And it's not so easy to look happy either, with your eyes shut. I—I had the loveliest dream. Of course I have forgotten what it was all about; I always forget dreams. But perhaps I was just dreaming it when you looked at me."

"Perhaps. I'm afraid it's one of the things we aren't going to know for certain."

"Did you——" Joyce paused irresolutely. "No, nothing," she added. "Have some more strawberries?"

Mervyn laughed a little. "Yes, I did," he said. "I hope it didn't wake you. I tried not to wake you."

"No, it didn't wake me. I'm glad. How on earth did you know what I was going to ask you? I only said two words of it."

"Your eyes said the rest."

"Joyce," he added presently, rising from the table, "do you think we are going to church this morning?"

Joyce also rose. She walked to the window and looked out. "I feel quite sure that we are going to church this evening; but this morning is too fine, and it would be too hot in church. I think we will go out into the open air and sit down somewhere. You shall take a book with you, and the cooler of the two—whichever it may be—shall read to the hotter."

"Which way shall we go?" asked Mervyn, as shortly afterward they passed through the garden gate out on to the high-road.

"Up on to the hills. It will suit a queer kind of exaltation that I'm feeling this morning. I suppose it is because it is such glorious weather."

"Yes; it's a magic morning."

"Magic! That's just the word for it. It changes everything; quite common things do not seem common any longer. Look at that golden broom there with the light on it, just on the edge of the heath. It's the ordinariest golden broom, but it's simply beautiful, and I love it—I could kiss it."

"Do," said Mervyn. "I'm not going to be jealous of a wretched vegetable; and there's no one coming. Do, by all means."

"It wouldn't be a very sane sort of thing to do, I own; but then that's where the magic comes in. It's all the weather; now yesterday——"

She stopped short. She had only been intending to speak of yesterday's weather, but yesterday did not stand speaking about, or even thinking about, just yet.

They went up the hill-side. The bracken was waist-high—a sea of pale green rippling to the slightest wind. Below its graceful stems lay the old bracken, brown and faded. On the fine sand of the pathway a thousand tiny insects hurried to and fro. Joyce had gathered two or three wild white roses from a hedge that they had passed, and was fastening them affectionately in her dress. In the distance they could hear the church bells just beginning; they sounded more sweetly and more musically than when one heard them in the village street; indeed, they suggested distance, far-awayness, remoteness; they awoke in Joyce a feeling of sad longing, the "desiderium" of the Latins, the "πόθος" of the Greeks—a feeling for which a more prosaic nation has no one exact word. For a time the two walked on in silence; then they sat down in the shadow; a fallen tree seemed to have fallen on purpose for their convenience. And because Joyce was a little tired with her walk, it was Mervyn who read; his voice was low and monotonous. Perhaps he was almost too careful not to be declamatory; but his reading was intelligent. It was rather a sad story that he was reading; these were the last words of it:

"Not only was his character entirely cleared. It was thought that he had undergone very much, and had done so for a very noble motive. He was admired—indeed, almost worshipped; and his book brought him fresh honor; it was praised everywhere and bought everywhere; almost every post brought him letters from people of whom he had never heard before, telling him of the pleasure or the consolation that they had found in his work. He had won reputation and the love of many. He had wealth now, and the life of ease and luxury was possible to him. That was why in all the city there was not one as unhappy as he."

There was, perhaps, some truth in this. The man in the story had missed the one thing that he wanted most; and the gain of the other things that he had always wanted so much less was only another bitterness to him. There was some truth in it, because after all we are the merest children, and if we cannot have just what we want, we are very much inclined to say that we will not play, and to sulk in a corner.

Joyce had heard the story before, and she liked it at times. In more critical moments she could see that it was wanting in brightness and strenuity. The author of it was very young, and had not learned that you must have a light to see the darkness by. But the story fitted her present mood; it seemed to suit their height above the village and their sense of distance. It is hard to sympathize with the sorrows to which one is nearest. Yet it was not a morning on which Joyce could stay long in the air of sorrowful sentimentality; her thoughts strayed from the sad story to other and happier things. Mervyn had put the book down and was stretched at her feet; he was rolling a cigarette and taking a lazy man's trouble about it; he lit it and smoked for some time in silence. All manner of quaint little summer sounds were going on around them—chirp and twitter, flutter of wings, buzzing of insects, rustle of branches.

Presently he happened to look up into his

wife's face. "Joyce," he said, "can you tell
me what you were thinking about then?"

She hesitated a second, and then looked away
from him. "No, dear, I don't think I can tell
you. Why?"

"Because you had that look again—the new
look—that you had when I kissed you in your
sleep this morning."

"This morning—this magic morning," she
echoed softly. "No, it's not only the weather;
I don't know what it is."

They walked home, back to the white cottage,
in silence. On Sunday they dined in the middle of the day because it suited Anna Martha
better; in merely material matters they generally
arranged themselves as might suit Anna Martha best. The afternoon passed drowsily away;
Joyce read books in a hammock that was
stretched between two trees in the garden at
the back of the house; Mervyn smoked many
cigarettes and went for a short walk. And in
the evening they went to church; it was not an
evening on which either of them was in a mood
to criticise very severely. The curate meant to
be quite right; so did the choir of village boys;
so did the organ, a very poor instrument. They
all meant to be quite right, and the rest did not
seem to matter very much.

Later in the evening Joyce played the piano
for Mervyn, and he sat and watched her.

She looked very sweet and delicate in the candle-light. She was playing from memory, and her thoughtful eyes were half closed. Her hands, moving over the keys, were small and white and beautiful. Outside, beyond the trees, one could see the crescent moon in a sky that was still thinking about the daylight that had gone but an hour ago. The music that she had been playing had suited well the fall of night, and the recollection of worship, and all gentle thoughts. She paused a moment, and then began to play the second movement of Beethoven's E-minor Sonata, the converse of the lovers. He waited until she had finished, and then he spoke:

"Joyce, dearest, I don't know how it happened, but yesterday I did not love you. It won't ever happen again. I love you now."

Joyce looked down at her hands, resting on the keys. There were tears in her eyes. "I knew," she said, almost in a whisper, "and I did not love you then."

"And now?"

"Very—very much." She put out the candles at the piano, and in a moment she was close to him in the dusk, with her head upon his shoulder. "Mervyn, my dear husband," she said, "I—I've got something to tell you."

8

MY LADY'S LILIES

"THEY'RE full of graciousness," you said
Of lilies in your garden growing.
"And you," I answered, "you are like
The fairest lily blowing."

To you the simile was naught;
It was too trite—it did not strike you.
But weren't the lilies mad with joy
At hearing they were like you!

VII

"JADIS"

OVER the flat fen country there were white mists rising. It was already growing dusk, but it was not going to be very dark this summer night. The weeds had been cut, and drifted down stream in thick masses. A thin middle-aged man stood by the lock-gates, watching an approaching boat. He was dressed in country clothes, but he had not the air of a country-man; he was pale and had a look of experience. Save for the regular sound of the sculls, every-thing was quite still. Save for the man at the lock-gates and the solitary occupant of the boat, there was no one in sight. It was a wide, flat, desolate scene.

The boat was rather a heavy tub, and the man who was sculling was tired and out of temper. As a rule he was thought to be a dis-tinctly brilliant and genial young man; but he wanted to get on to Nunnisham, which was five miles beyond the lock, that night, and he had been considerably delayed by the weeds. The gods had given him extraordinarily good

looks and many other good things, enough to
keep him genial unless, as on the present occa-
sion, circumstances tried him severely.   At the
lock he drew into the bank and hailed the middle-aged man who still stood watching him.

"Hi! what are the weeds like above the lock?"

"Very bad, sir."   The answer was given in
a serious, respectful voice.

The young man swore gently to himself.   "Is
there any place near here where I could put up
for the night?"   .

"There is only a public-house, sir.   I am the
landlord of it—my name is Hill.   I could give
you a bedroom; a little rough, perhaps, but——"

"Good—a bed and some supper—capital!
That is the only bit of luck I've had to-day."
As he was speaking the young man picked up
a small knapsack which was lying in the stern
of the boat and jumped out.   He made the boat
fast, and joined the landlord on the towing-path.

"It is this way.   You will allow me to carry
that for you, sir."

As they walked along, the brilliant young
man—his name was Philip Vince—chatted
freely.   He was taking a holiday up the river,
and was to have joined a friend at Nunnisham
that night and then gone on with him the day
after.   He told the landlord all this, and also
surmised that Hill was not a native of the fen
country.

"No, sir," was the answer. "I was valet to Sir Charles Sulmont. You have perhaps heard of him."

Philip had never heard of him, but said that he had.

"When Sir Charles died he left me a little money, and I married a maid who was then in Lady Sulmont's service. I bought this house with a little assistance from her ladyship, and settled here. I was very young then, and I have been here eighteen years."

Philip gathered from further talk as they went along that Mrs. Hill was dead, and that she had left one child, Jeanne, a girl of seventeen, who lived with her father. When they reached the inn, Hill showed Philip a bedroom —a large, comfortable room, and began to make some apology about supper. They very rarely had any one staying in the house, and there was nothing but—— Here Philip interrupted:

"You would be doing me a kindness if you would let me have supper with you and your daughter. I hate solitude. I mean, if your— if Miss Hill wouldn't object."

"If you really wish it, sir, I should be very pleased; so also, I am sure, would Jeanne." Hill was a born valet; he had the manner; if he had lived out of service for a hundred years, he would have been a valet still. When Hill left him, Philip looked round the room and

congratulated himself. Everything was very
neat and clean. The landlord was a capital
fellow—a little solemn, perhaps, but still a capital fellow. This was far above the accommoda-
tion which he had expected.

Just then a light footfall came up the stairs,
and Philip caught a snatch of a French song.
The song stopped short just before the footfall
passed his door. Philip conjectured that this
must be the daughter, and that it had been a
French maid that Hill had married; hence the
name Jeanne and that snatch of song. Also
that the daughter had been warned of his arrival, and had gone to put on her prettiest
dress. All of these conjectures were quite correct. And yet when Jeanne entered the sitting-
room a few minutes afterward and saw Philip
for the first time, she was so startled that she
showed it slightly. Philip was also a little surprised, for a different reason, and did not show
it at all. He had thought of the possibility
that Jeanne might be pretty; and she was a
beauty—a brunette, childlike in many ways,
but with a woman's eyes. Her voice was
good, and her first few words showed that she
had had some education.

It took her about ten minutes to get from decided shyness to complete confidence. Philip
was feeling far too good-tempered to let any one
be shy with him; he made Hill and his daugh-

ter talk, and he talked freely himself. He liked
the simplicity of everything about him; he had
grown tired of formalities in London. He liked
cold beef and salad, for he was very hungry, and
—yes, above all, he liked Jeanne. What on
earth were that face and that manner doing in
a riverside inn? She was perfect; she did not
apologize too much, did not get flurried, did
not have red hands, spoke correctly, laughed
charmingly — in a word, was bewitching.
Really, he was glad that he had been prevented
from going on to Nunnisham. Toward the end
of supper, he discovered that she was wearing
a white dress with forget-me-nots in it.

The table was cleared by a native servant, who
seemed all red cheeks and new boots. Hill
went off to superintend the business of the inn.
Philip was left alone with Jeanne. She told
him to smoke, and he was obedient; he also
made her tell him other things.

Yes, she had been to school at Nunnisham—
rather too good a school for her, she was afraid;
but her mother had wished it. Her mother
had taught her French and a little music.
Music and drawing were the best things, she
thought; but she liked *some* books. She owned
that it was lonely, sometimes, at the inn. "I
am glad you came," she confessed frankly.

"Jeanne," said Philip, "I heard you humming a line or two of 'Jadis' before supper,

didn't I? I wish you would sing it to me."
She agreed at once, crossing the room to a little
cottage piano—rather a worn-out instrument,
but still a piano. The melody — plaintive,
gentle, childish—of Jeanne's sweet voice, and
the sadness of the words, with their quaint, pen-
sive refrain, did not miss their effect.

> "Je n'attends plus rien ici-bas;
> Bonheur perdu ne revient pas,
> Et mon cœur ne demande au ciel
> Qu'un repos éternel."

He thanked her; he had liked that very
much. "Why," he added, "were you startled
when you saw me?"

"Because you are a dream come true. I saw
your face in a dream last night—as clearly as I
see you now. All this time I have been feeling
as if I had known you before."

"Really?" he said. He had not quite believed
it. "How many things come true! One says
things about the shortness of time or the certainty of death so often that they lose all meaning; then when one grows old or lies dying, the
platitudes get to have terrible force—they come
true."

She was struck by that; she kept her eyes
fixed on his, and he went on talking to her. He
did not, as the time wore on, always mean
quite so much as he said; and she meant much

more than she said. That is a common difference between a man and a woman on such occasions. It seemed to her that now for the first
time she really lived.

After Jeanne had said good-night, Philip
had some chat with her father about her.

"I expect that she will be engaged very soon,
sir," he said; "a young man called Banks—
William Banks—is anxious, and has spoken to
me; and she likes him."

"Now, I wonder," thought Philip to himself
as he went upstairs, "why she never even hinted
that to me. 'M—yes, I see."

Next morning after breakfast he went away,
taking with him a few forget-me-nots, a pleasant
memory, and just the faintest possible feeling
of remorse. They all faded.

.   .   .   .

Jeanne had seemed so quiet and depressed of
late that her father, in order to cheer her up,
had invited Mr. William Banks to spend the
evening.

Mr. Banks was a small shopkeeper in Nunnisham, and considered to be no mean wag by
those who knew him. Yet he felt unable to
cheer her up. "Supposing we had a bit of a
toon, Jenny," he suggested at last. She was
quite docile. She played one thing after another. Suddenly she began "Jadis."

"I don't understand French myself," Mr.

Banks remarked, "but the words of a song don't matter." She had never thought much about the words herself before. But now?

"Depuis qu'il a trahi sa foi
Rien n'a plus de charme pour moi."

Her voice faltered a little, but she sang on to the end of the verse:

"Et mon cœur ne demande au ciel
Qu'un repos éternel."

Yes, the song had "come true." Just there she gave way and began to cry a little.

A week afterward Mr. Banks announced that his attentions to Miss Hill were at an end.

THE BIRD CAGE

THERE is a cage of many a bird
    Hung up in space by Natural Law;
Doves coo, the peacock is absurd,
    Swans sing and die, and black rooks caw;
The fighting cock is killed or wins,
    Peewits peewit, and pouters pout;
The ostrich feeds on sardine tins,
    And they can none of them get out.
That's what the noise is all about;
    They want to, but they can't get out.

The cage has many thousand bars;
    Each bar's a scientific fact;
Through these they watch the shooting stars,
    And get emotion from the act.
But one owl says the stars aren't there,
    But in the eyes that watch them fall;
" And eyes, however fine a pair,
    Don't as a fact exist at all.
These bars that make our prison wall
    Are but phenomena—that's all."

That doesn't stop them, not a bit;
  The skylark sings, and beats his breast
Against a bar, and stunned by it,
  Drops down to die and to protest.
As panting in the cage he lies,
  The glory of a shooting star
Drops splendor down the dazzled skies,
  Where dreams and their cloud-chambers are.
"And oh," he cries, "to fly so far
  Where dreams and bright star-glories are!"

"Tu-whit! the little brute is dead;
  That will be one star-gazer less."
These are the words the great owl said;
  The others cry, "Oh, yes! oh, yes!"
But one sweet-voiced and golden brown
  Croons o'er the lark a plaintive song:
"Though the claws are crossed and the wings
      droop down,
  And the breast is still, it is not for long.
His voice was sweet and his wings were strong,
  Surely he will awake ere long."

"Quite right," the duck quacks, "there are
      germs
  Of life when life seems wholly gone.
The lark will do to feed the worms,
  And worms are good to feed upon."
"That's splendid!" all the owls reply,
  "Our life from death its substance draws;
A skylark should be glad to die,

And make us fat by Natural Laws.
You and the rooks with their First Caws,
Are getting on in Natural Laws."

Ages are past, the cage is there,
But now to suffocation packed,
The dying cry for light and air,
With quavering notes that thirst has cracked.
The living beat against the bars,
Bedewed with tears, begrimed with jest,
In mad desire to join the stars,
To fly away and be at rest.
The down falls from their wounded breast;
They die—and no one knows the rest.

VIII

THE DOG THAT GOT FOUND

THERE was a dog once that got to be utterly sick of conventionality. It lived in a great house, had proper exercise, proper food, a proper control over its temper, and everything quite proper. And after a time things got so bad that it made its complaint to the butler, who had condescended to take it out with him a short way. And this is what the dog said to the butler:

"O beautiful butler, I am a-weary, a-weary! Why should I bark whenever I hear the front-door bell ring, and have it imputed unto me for intelligence? For I know in my heart that the visitors at this house are respectable visitors. I know that they will not steal the spoons, or murder my master and mistress, or growl at you, O beautiful butler. Why then should I bark at them and frighten them? It is such a paltry farce. Why should I pretend to be devoted to my master and mistress? I like them well enough; but they are quite ordinary people, and I am most emphatically *not* devoted to

them. Yet I let them believe it. My master
thinks that when he dies I shall fetch a Sir-Ed-
win-Landseerish artist, to show my instinct,
and then die oleographically on his tombstone to
show my fidelity. Bah! Why should I lie
down when I am told, and get up when I am
told, and always be sent off to bed at the same
time? Why should I pretend to be surprised
and piggishly pleased, whenever I have any
food given me? I tell you that I'm the slave
of conventionality, and I hate it. Let us be
natural! For the love of bones let us be natural!
Liberty, O beautiful butler, and Fraternity, and
Equality!"

The dog stopped, gasping. To the butler it
was only a noise that the dog was making, an
unintelligible noise. For the butler could not
understand doggish; moreover, on that morning he had been rendered unhappy by circumstances, and he was in no mood to tolerate the
yelping of a fox-terrier.

"Look here, master Fido," he said severely.

"Sickly, sentimental name it is, too," interrupted the dog.

"Look here, master Fido," the butler re-
sumed, more severely. "If you can't close
your head, I shall just take you back again.
That's what I shall do with *you*. Here am I.
I gets my eyes cursed by master Frederick for
what's not my fault nor anybody else's fault

except his own. I expect that—and I put up with it. And very likely I'm a worm, a trodden worm, being treated as such. But I am *not* going to be yelped at by no fox-terriers. Human nature draws the line somewhere."

"A stupid man, although beautiful," the dog thought to himself, as he silently took his place at the butler's heels. And when he got home he went straight to his bed, and dreamed of a free artistic life, full of love-stories.

On the following day a large tom-cat was brought to the house. It had come from a beautiful home for lost culture in South Kensington. Fido discovered that it was expected that he would fight with the cat; so he at once made friends with it to show his originality, and he explained to it how this kind of life hurt him, and how hungry his soul was. Now the cat was very high-toned and as full of other people's phrases as it could stick.

"Ah, yes!" it murmured with a tired mew. "You revolt. It is so very *fin de siècle* to revolt. And you would live? I do not see the necessity; that goes without saying, since I am a quietist. It is almost more *fin de siècle* to be a quietist, you know. You don't know? Ah, how right of you! Never know. Only imagine—dream. There are rose-leaves in the world, and old silver and beautiful women, and wind-songs and sea-songs. Go and look for them. Go out into the cool night, when it is dark, and you can see nothing, and look for them. You're drinking my milk, you pig."

The last remark, which—as compared with the rest—was plain, was unfortunately also true. Fido had done it from absence of mind, and he was sore ashamed. But he liked the way the cat talked; it did seem so very high. So that night he made unto himself an opportunity, and got away from the great house. And first of all he careered into Piccadilly. There he sat down in the middle of the road, scratched his head with his hind-foot, and said, "O my adventurous soul!"

At that moment a passing cab nearly ran over Fido, and the driver flicked him with his whip. It was painful.

"This is life," said Fido to himself, "poignant and intense, it is true, but still quite free from conventionality. I shall come to the sweetness and brightness of it presently. But—lovely Helen!—how that whip did hurt!"

He was a moderately intelligent dog, and he saw that these crowded thoroughfares were irksome to a dog that wanted to be soulful and not to take the trouble to see where it was going. The desert—the sandy, lonely, wind-swept desert—would do him far better. So he stopped a large St. Bernard, which was taking its mas-

9

ter out, and inquired which was the way to the nearest desert.

"Go home, you flighty-headed young idiot," said the St. Bernard sternly.

Fido walked on, determined to take no notice of this insult; but his angry soul bubbled and boiled within him, and called for vengeance until he could stand it no longer. "I must punish that dog," he said to himself; "I'll go back and bark at his tail, and then run away. He's chained to a man, so he won't be able to run after me."

So he went back and barked most nobly; unfortunately he barked at the wrong dog, who was not chained, and when he ran away the wrong dog ran after him, being wishful to eat a portion of him. And for a long time Fido ran on, going westward, and then southwestward, skirting passionate Brompton, and pausing at last in the North End Road. But his pursuer had run into a lamp-post that stood in the parts about Knightsbridge, and so had gone no further, being sorry for himself.

In the North End Road Saturday night is market-night, and there is such cheapness in that road as can only be found in one other part of great London. It was Saturday night when Fido got there, and the street was crowded. The flare of the lights on the barrows, the hoarse cries of the salesmen, the hurry of everybody, and the excessive intoxication of the three people nearest him, flurried Fido. He found, however, something which was very like a small desert under a barrow where peppermint rock was being sold at a price which, the proprietor explained, barely paid for the paper in which it was wrapped. At the next stall was a very scientific-looking old gentleman in a dressing-gown, a gray beard, and a college cap. Fido sat in his miniature desert and listened to the old gentleman, who was addressing the crowd:

"It was my aim, therefore, bein' a philosopher as well as a scientist, to go a little further than this Edising what discovered electricity. The question which I arst myself, and which I arsks you to-night, was simply this—why should I die? Why should I not use some modification of this electricity, combinin' it with other things, to restore my wasted vitality and prolong my life? For this purpose I studied for several years in three forrun capitals, and the results is the little machine you see before you. You grasps the two 'andles in your two 'ands, and say when the shock's as strong as you care to 'ave it. 'Appiness and 'ealth for one penny! 'Appiness and 'ealth by the newly invented life-improver for one penny a shock. After to-night the price will be one guinea a shock, so now's your chance."

"This is better," Fido thought to himself. "We never had any brilliant theories and new discoveries in that horrible abode of conventionality where they made me do trust-and-paid-for."

At this moment the dog noticed a butcher's shop on the other side of the pavement. The butcher himself stood at one side of it, with the agony of a great soul written on his fat face, speaking to the crowd with the earnestness and conviction of a dying man to dying men:

"(*Prestissimo*) Buy, buy, buy! (*Adagio con molto expressione*) Lyedy, gentle lyedy, 'ere's a Sunday dinner for yer. Make your own price, lyedy, and we cuts to suit yer. (*Rallentando*) Gentle lyedy, to-morrer's Sunday."

"This is Fraternity and Equality," thought Fido. And then another of those curious fits of absence of mind came over him, and he came out from under the barrow, and went over to the butcher's shop; he made a small selection, and walked away with the selection in his mouth. But the butcher saw him, and his voice rose like the wail of a lost spirit: "Blanks and initialled hyphens! kick that dorg, some of yer!"

And then it seemed to Fido that earthquakes, explosions, volcanoes, and empty meat tins were all happening at once, and that in the middle of them he himself was running in three different

directions simultaneously. When he collected
his thoughts again he was limping along in
great pain on the darker side of the Fulham
Road, having dropped the selection into the
mud, and feeling like to die. He paused on
Putney Bridge to make a moral reflection, addressed to no one in particular: " When you
forsake the paths of conventionality keep your
eye upon your fleshy appetites. Never forget
that you were not made wholly spiritual."

He crawled with infinite difficulty up Putney
Hill. It had grown very late now, and there
was no one about. He was cut, and bruised,
and broken, plastered with mud and blood.
When a dog means to do a pathetic thing, it
likes to do it in private. So Fido crept away
to the right on to Putney Common, and there
he hid himself under a bush, panting, with his
tongue out. He prayed in faltering doggish
that it might occur to a stream of clear, cool
water to come past him, because he was too tired
to go in search of it. In the early hours he
heard a kind of singing in his ears; and at first
his wandering mind thought that this must be
his mistress practising her scales in the room
overhead; and then he remembered that there
was no room overhead, nothing but darkness,
and then again it might possibly be the sound
of the cool stream coming toward him. He
waited a little longer, but the stream did not

come; there was only one thing left to do, and he did it—in a simple and unaffected manner.

.   .   .   .

The laboring man noticed the body, as he took his short cut across the common. " Bill," he said to his mate, " 'ere's a dead dorg, with a silver collar to 'im; 'e must 'ave got lorst."

As a matter of fact he had just got found, and his soul was chasing ghost-rats in the happy hunting-grounds. "Fair doos with the collar," remarked Bill.

THE BAT AND THE DEVIL

I

THE bat he hung on the yew-tree bough,
As the devil came over the high hill brow.
He opened the gate of the grim churchyard,
And cursed at the hinges that went so hard.
He sat him down 'neath the same yew-tree
And long at the poor little bat glared he:
"It is but a leaf that is hanging there,
Dead, but moved by the strong sweet air.
Plants and trees are nothing to me,
And nothing to Him who made them be.
They have one life and no more than that"—
                                        Poor old Bat!

II

The bat dropped down from the yew-tree spray,
And crawled on the devil in a grewsome way.
A woman's skin would have leaped with fear
At the cold claws touching there and here;
But the devil did naught but chuckle and sing:
"It's a creeping thing! It's a creeping thing!
By the Serpent of Eden, first of the line,
All that creeps on the earth is mine.

This is no leaf, but a soul to crawl
In my inner chamber along the wall,
With the poison-snake and the snail of slime
In hell's dark place that knows not time,
For my sisters to mock and be merry at "—
Poor old Bat!

III

But the grim churchyard grew dusk and dark,
And stars 'gan twinkling, spark by spark;
And out and away on the air of night
Sailed the bat with a noiseless flight,
With scarce a whirr of its nervous wing,
As it wheeled around in a widening ring;
But a curse came into the devil's eyes,
And his mouth was red with blasphemies:
"By the angels that float in the heavenly air,
By the holy sheen of the wings they wear—
And damned be they forevermore!
All that flies in the air will soar
Upward to Him, and away from me!"

.   .   .   .

And the lightning blasted the grim yew-tree,
And the thunder roared, and the rain made foam
On the path, as the devil got him home—
Home by the broad road and the level—
Poor old Devil!

IX

TWO POETS

"Now, look here, Hubert, do just let me read you the finest part."

There was something splendid in the vanity of this large, venerable man. He was only middle-aged, but he looked venerable. He sat well back in his easy-chair, full of complacency and dinner. His fat, white, ringed fingers toyed delicately with his liqueur-glass. His eyes, as he spoke, glanced lovingly toward an awful portfolio—a portfolio as bulgy as its owner—which rested on a writing-table in a far corner. He was so childish and eager that Hubert felt that it was impossible to be angry with this fatuous poet, although it would be still more impossible to listen to his verses. Hubert was five years younger than the venerable Archibald, and looked ten years younger. He had the broad, low brow and the luminous eyes that see the humor of things. They had been friends at college, and college friendships stick.

They only resembled one another in the fact

that they both wrote verses. Archibald was a
fairly rich man, and was about to publish his
own works at his own expense in dainty vellum
binding. Hubert, although not poor, was
much poorer, and quite unpublished. Archibald had never suffered a strong passion, had
no strange experiences, and no close ties of affection; for he had many acquaintances and
no near relations. In Archibald's affections,
Hubert had told him more than once, Archibald himself and his own verses came first,
sweet champagne and oily liquors second,
chocolate bon-bons third, and the rest nowhere.
At which Archibald would smile a fat smile,
and say that he was quite prepared to own his
devotion to his art. He was so perfectly well
satisfied with himself that the laughter or jeers
of his friend never affected him, and would not
have affected him even if they had not been—
as they were—always uttered good-humoredly.
Hubert had been less fortunate than Archibald.
He was more sensitive and less sensible. He
was susceptible, and had been the fool of more
than one woman. At this time he was married, but separated from his wife. He was re-
served on such points, and Archibald never
knew that his friend was, or ever had been,
married. Hubert was always suffering the remorse that he was always causing himself; and
yet his frailties were lovable, and he had never

lost his sweet temper and his geniality. His
experiences and sorrows had gone straight
through his heart out into his verse. In verse
he had found much consolation, but no money.
It was not poverty that caused either of the
two to write. Vanity compelled Archibald;
the desire for comfort moved Hubert.

Yet with all their differences they remained
very good friends. They often dined together,
as they had been dining now, in Archibald's
chambers. On rare occasions Hubert would
allow Archibald to have recourse to the awful
portfolio; then Archibald was happy. Hubert
never read his own poetry aloud, and his friend
only knew that he had written some verses for
which he had not been able to find a publisher.

"Now, my dear fellow," said Archibald, re-
peating his request, "I value your opinion.
The part I want to read you is the first twenty
lines of 'The Darkness of Eros.' After that,
if you don't want to hear any more, I promise
to stop. I read those twenty lines to Smithson, and he asked me to go on; and you know
Smithson's not the man to be easily pleased."
Archibald rose and waddled toward the portfolio like a frightened hen getting home.

"All nonsense, old man," said Hubert;
"you'd had Smithson to dinner."

"But that's nothing to do with it," replied

Archibald, fumbling with a bundle of proofs
which he had selected from the portfolio.

"Well, you know, Smithson's mostly used
to dining at restaurants, and he can't quite understand a free feed. I can. I like it. But
Smithson always has an idea that he's got to
pay for his dinner somehow. When he dines
with one, he always admires the pictures and
furniture. Of course, he can't admire your
Landseers; because, although Smithson's vulgar, he's not so hopeless as all that. But he
praises your poetry instead."

Archibald smoothed out one long slip on his
plump knee. "Now it's just precisely because
by a remark like that you show a certain
amount of insight that Smithson doesn't pos-
sess that I want you to—er—now then."

And before Hubert could stop him he had
read the first line:

"'Shall we sing of the sea-foam that bore thee, the
    Mother of Love?'"

"Next line ends in 'dove,'" remarked Hubert
waywardly.

"It does *not*," said Archibald emphatically.
"It ends in 'above.' And you might have
had 'grove' or 'shove,' or heaps of things.
You spoil it, you know, by talking like that."

"No, my dear fellow," said Hubert; "it's
Smithson who really spoils you. Look here.

When you read your verses I want to laugh, and that's not right. I'll tell you what I'll do. I'll do something I never did for you before. I'll take that proof home and read it, and give you my detailed opinion of it."

"You will?" said Archibald, and his eyes brightened as he handed him the proof. "I'm not sure that it would not be better for me to read it; but, on my word, it's something that you want to read it yourself when you've only heard one line." For it was Archibald's conviction that Hubert must have been attracted by that line to make the proposal. "And you'll give me your opinion of it," he continued, "your candid opinion—just what you think, you know?"

"I will," said Hubert; "but you will publish it just the same, whatever my opinion is."

"I own that," replied Archibald blandly: "because I have a confidence in that work which I am persuaded is just."

"And talking of candid opinions," Hubert went on, with the plain speaking of a very old friend, "this particular mixture of citron and treacle is rather more nasty than I care for. I know it's your taste, but——"

Archibald smiled and touched the bell. Then they fell to talking of the wickedness of wine merchants and publishers and of the beauty of old college-days, until the small hours. Hubert was thinking as his cab took him back to his own chambers. He was thinking of a certain ship of his which had recently come in and which he had long before given up. It would enable him, if he liked, to do precisely what Archibald was doing—to publish his own verses at his own expense.

On the table in his chambers he found a letter waiting for him, addressed to him in a familiar feminine hand. It was written on thick, rough-edged paper, and bore a great gilt monogram. She was always adopting fashions, he knew, but they took time in reaching her. There were three sheets, all crossed; and one of them was smeared with cigarette ashes. He glanced through them impatiently and flung them on the fire. Then he took out his check-book, wrote a check, and put it in an envelope, which he stamped and addressed.

Then he went to bed with the pleasant consciousness that the ship which had come in had now gone out again; and that the poems would have to wait.

Yet they ultimately found a publisher.

. . . .

Archibald Somers and Hubert Ray both died in the same year. Sixty years afterward a critical work appeared on Archibald Somers. As this critical work expressed what were certainly the general sentiments of the time, some of it may be quoted.   Besides, it is a little curious:

"It is to be regretted that Hubert Ray had not the
humility to undertake the work of Boswell for Johnson; although he was undoubtedly less than Boswell,
even as Somers was undoubtedly greater than Johnson.
Had he done so, we might have had a clearer picture
of the personality of the finest English poet since Mil-
ton.   As it is, Archibald Somers is an indistinct figure; a figure which we love and reverence, but of
which we would fain know more.   Hubert Ray was
too much taken up with his own filthy intrigues, his
own morbid rhymes and spiteful lampoons; he was too
much blinded by conceit to see the greatness of his
intimate friend.   It is a satire on their times that Hubert Ray should have found a publisher foolish enough
to produce his works for nothing, while Archibald
Somers positively had to pay to give the world a work
which it now knows to be priceless.   It is true that
subsequently, even in their life-time, the pre-emi-
nence of Somers was acknowledged; but if we may
judge the man from the delicacy of his writing, his
modesty would be astounded if he knew—alas, he can
never know!—the position which he justly holds now
among the poets of this land."

AINIGMATA

I WANTED the sweep of the wild wet weather,
  The wind's long lash and the rain's free fall,
The toss of the trees as they swayed together,
  The measureless gray that was over them all;
Whose roar speaks more than a language spoken;
  Wordless and wonderful, cry on cry—
The sob of an earth that is vexed and broken,
  The answering sob of a broken sky.

What could they tell us? We see them ever—
  The trees, and the sky, and the stretch of the
    land;
But they give us a word of their secret never;
  They tell no story we understand.
Yet haply the ghost-like birch out yonder
  Knows much in a placid and silent way;
The rain might tell what the gray clouds ponder,
  The winds repeat what the violets say.

Why weeps the rain? Do you know its sorrow?
  Do you know why the wind is so sad—so
    sad?

Have you stood in the rift 'twixt a day and a
    morrow,
  Seen their hands meet and their eyes grow
    glad?
Is the tree's pride stung at its top's abasement?
  Is the white rose more of a saint than the red?
What thinks the star as it sees through the
    casement   .
  A young girl lying, beautiful, dead?
   10

X

WHITE NIGHTS

1—THE STORY OF UNA AND ALTERA

LILIAS, the princess whom all loved, was ill and not able to sleep. We did not know just at first what was the matter with her, and indeed the court physicians owned that they did not understand her illness. The king, her father, was away at a conference in a distant island, and her two sisters, the Princesses Rosalys and Yseult, grew very anxious. Lilias had always been slight and delicate; and now every day she seemed to grow more pale and fragile and worn. A very little thing would be a burden to her and make her tired. Yet she kept her beauty; it seemed even to be increased, and there was a more pathetic meaning in her gray eyes. Her loveliness lay in her rare and wonderful spirituality. It was not the common beauty of a woman; it was the beauty that one would imagine in a saint—the reflection in her look of the beautiful soul within her.

To all around her she was as kind and gentle

as ever, but one could see that she had lost her interest in things. She would sit, looking out on the sunset or listening to the far-off sound of the sea, saying nothing. We knew that she had some sorrow, and we would have done much—anything—to have helped her; for she had many lovers, and she always seemed to win, even from quite ordinary men, the best love— the love that desires only to give and not to receive. But there was none who would have dared to ask for her confidence. It was very rarely that she spoke of herself. Most women will chatter about their hearts to other women, but the Princess Lilias was not like that. Her share of the more intimate sorrows and joys of humanity was so sacred that even sympathy was in peril of becoming profanation.

All this should have been nothing to me, the king's fool, the son of a scullion in the royal household, but it happened one night that Lilias said she would like some one to come and tell her stories from time to time, especially on those nights when she could not sleep. It was then that the chief minister told me to hold myself in readiness; he explained to me that he had no reason to believe I could make up stories myself, but he knew that I was well acquainted with the jests of all lands, and that I might, by drawing from the stores of my memory, be able to be amusing. I was not to tell sad stories. My audience was to consist of the three princesses, as a rule.

I mistrusted my own powers. The Princess Rosalys was quiet, kind, womanly, and I knew that she would not judge my attempts too hardly. Yseult was petulant, wayward, *provocante*, and sometimes bitter of spirit, although she was not able to hurt me. And it seemed impossible to make anything good enough for Lilias to hear; and yet I wanted to try. I was not going to obey the minister's orders and make my stories consist entirely of remembered jests; for it did not seem to me to be the best kind of sympathy to laugh with those that weep. Yes, I was glad that I was going to be with Lilias; I liked to look at her; indeed, I liked all beautiful and sorrowful things, being destined to ugliness and merriment all my days.

Those days will soon—very soon—be at an end now. For I who write these words am under sentence of death, and together with this account of the white nights of the Princess Lilias, I shall be writing the last chapter of my own story, showing how it was that I was condemned to die. Now, when I was first summoned, it was to the great hall, and the princesses were seated near the fire, for it was early in the summer and the nights were still chilly. Lilias was half reclining, looking tired and white, but with her gray eyes wide open. Rosalys was seated on the ground at her feet, her head resting on her sister's knees. But Yseult sat a little way apart, with laughing eyes, her fingers trembling on the strings of the harp which she had been playing.

"We await your story, fool," said the dark-haired Yseult.

"Will you tell us a story, Otho?" asked Ro-: salys more gently.

"A story of children," added Lilias; her voice was more musical and softer.

"Yes," I said, "but you must play for me a little while, Yseult, while I think." It was the privilege of the king's fool to be allowed absolution from all etiquette. It was generally felt that he did not matter, and I said what I would. "Will you play for me?"

She showed her little white teeth. "Why should I play for you, fool? Yes, I will," she added petulantly. "What shall it be?"

"Searching music—music that goes away to look—baffled music."

"But you are reasonable, fool. You ask a light thing—an easy thing."

. And, being wayward, she would not play as I had asked her. She made music that laughed and laughed; and suddenly it found out that all was too sad to laugh about, and went sobbing away and hid itself. She looked at me proudly when she had finished, knowing that she had played well and thinking that I would praise her. But I stood leaning against the high mantelpiece, with my eyes on the gray eyes of Lilias.

The silence was pleasant; pleasant too was the dim light and the fragrance of the logs that smouldered on the open hearth. For a moment I said nothing, and then—standing there—I began the story of Una and Altera.

.   .   .   .

Some people thought that Mark, the king of Mirage, was eccentric; others considered him to be wise; but to most he seemed brutal. He had a queer temper, soured, but with a streak of tenderness in it.

He would frequently make theories on the spur of the moment, which were not good; he also clung to them, as a rule, and acted upon them, which was still worse.

One day, when he was a young man and had not been long on the throne, he was talking to his chief counsellor. And the chief counsellor happened to say something on the subject of education. It was enough; it started Mark.

"No looking-glasses!" Mark said suddenly, "and no portraits! They are the ruin of all education, and 'Know thyself' is the worst advice that ever was given. Why am I self-conscious? Looking-glasses and portraits are the reason. Why are you—you will excuse me—

so outrageously affected? Once more—looking-glasses and portraits." For Mark was not
good-looking, but the chief counsellor had a
very fine open countenance.

The chief counsellor moved his shoulders
just a very little and made his eyebrows ex-
pressive.

"One must brush one's hair sometimes," he
said deprecatingly, "and without a looking-
glass——"

"I don't see the necessity," interrupted the
king. "Besides, with a little practice you can
do even that without a looking-glass. I *always*
brush my hair without a looking-glass." This
had been moderately obvious, but the chief
counsellor did not like to allude to it. "When
I am married and have a son," the king went
on, "I will not allow him even to know of the
existence of such things as looking-glasses or
portraits. He shall never see his own face until his character is formed."

"Were you thinking of getting married?"
asked the chief counsellor, by way of changing the subject.

"I was."

"Might I—" the chief counsellor hesitated—
"might I ask if you have already honored
any woman with your love?"

"You might, but it has nothing to do with
it. Immortals! You don't think I would

marry any woman that I really loved. Would
you drink Lafite out of a stable-bucket? "

"No, but I should like to own enough of it to
last me my life-time."

"And marriage does *not* last a life-time,"
the king broke in impetuously. "Love does,
if you don't marry. Marriage, sooner or later,
at the best changes love into that nauseous
wholesome affection you have for your dog or
your father. Oh, you're an ordinary person!
You simply *daren't* be new."

The chief counsellor might have retorted
that the king "simply daren't" be anything
else. But he did not. He sighed and withdrew.

Shortly afterward the king acted on one of
his theories. He married a woman he did not
love in the least. He told her so. "I like you
because you're fairly pretty and good-tempered,"
he said. "I don't love you, and I never shall,
because our souls don't touch at any point.
You couldn't possibly love me, because I happen to be horrible in most ways. But business
is business. You probably would like to be a
queen, and I have the vacancy to offer. To-
day week would suit me very well. If you've
any engagement for that day don't mind saying so, and I'll find somebody else."

Curiously enough, this particular woman did
love Mark—loved him very badly. It is still

more curious, seeing that she loved him, that
she should have married him after such a proposal as this. " But," she thought, " I will never
let him see that I love him until I have made
him love me." She never did let him find
out her love for him, and, as a natural consequence, he never loved her; a little less nobility
would have made her happier. After a year
she bore him a daughter and died, and King
Mark walked up and down the long gallery outside the room where she was lying dead, curs-
ing his dead wife and all women, for he had
greatly desired to have a son.

He bade the women of the palace to take
charge of the child and call her Una. He gave
minute instructions about her education; she
was never to see the reflection of herself in a
mirror, or polished metal, or water; there were
to be no pictures whatever in the rooms where
she lived. She was not to know that there
were any such things. His orders were carried
out with exactitude. People mostly had a
habit of obeying King Mark. For seven years
the king never saw his daughter: he went
away to the wars, and absolutely refused to sit
in a tent of cloth-of-gold three miles away from
the scene of action, drinking sack and being
styled Most Puissant. That kind of thing did
not amuse him; he wanted fighting. He was
not a good swordsman, but he came out safely

from all his battles. "You have brought back
your life and your honor," said the chief counsellor. "And I do not want either," answered
King Mark. "I only want one thing, and I
shall never have it."

One day he suddenly entered that wing of
the house where his daughter Una lived. He
was shown the room where she was; he opened
the door and entered. She had no dolls, because they were considered to be contrary to the
spirit of the king's regulations. She was reading in a big illuminated missal, for she had no
companions and no games, and had been all
her time learning things. The illuminations
had been very carefully selected. There was
no butterfly, nor bird, nor flower depicted there-
in. The king sat down with his elbows on
his knees and his chin in his hands, looking
at her. She was very beautiful; there was
sunlight in her hair; there was sunlight in her
eyes; her smile was sunlight. As soon as she
saw the king she put the missal aside, and
without the least shyness or embarrassment
came toward him. She took both his hands in
her own and kissed him. "You are my dearest Mark," she said, "and I have never seen
you before. They have told me of you. You
have been away fighting. That is grand. The
more you fight the more I will love you."

King Mark was enraptured. He was especially pleased that Una called him by his name and not by the commonplace style of the commonplace relationship. He stayed a long time with her, and found her most bright and affectionate and free from self-consciousness. He told her stories and she told him stories in return, using free dramatic gestures. "Now I must go, Una," he said at last. "Is there anything I can do for you—anything you want?"

"You, you and your stories," she answered. "You tell them as if you hated people and wanted to fight them, and it's grand."

So the king went away madly exalted. In the corridor he met the grave chief counsellor.

"Counsellor," he cried joyously, "is there anything in the world that you want?"

"The Order of the Innermost has not yet been conferred upon me." This had always been a sore point with the chief counsellor.

"You shall have it," shouted the king, and passed on. He next met Una's governess. "Una's governess, tell me—is there anything in the world that you want?" he asked.

"Nothing, O king—nothing for myself. But, oh, that poor Una! That poor child!" and she burst into tears.

"Come with me and explain yourself," said the king. And he took her to the room where he never did any work, and which was consequently called his study. There the governess

explained. Una was so beautiful and had no
chance of knowing her own beauty—the greatest joy that child or woman can have. "And
I mayn't speak to her of it. Can't she have
just one looking-glass?" The king thought for
a moment and replied: "She shall have a large
looking-glass, and I will take her to see her
reflection in it. But you must go on as before
and never speak to her of such things."
"Thank you," said the governess. "Women
do *need* a looking-glass." She herself was as
ugly as an unromantic virtue.

On the following day the king had one end
of a little room entirely covered with looking-
glass. Four yards in front of the looking-glass
a silk cord was stretched across the room. He
had a fresh lock put on the door with a little
silver key to it. Then he bound over the work-
men to secrecy and went to find Una. "Una,"
he said, "I have a secret to tell you. It is not
generally known, but you are one of twins.
Your sister is rather like you, and I always
have her dressed exactly like you. Her name
is Altera."

"I have always wanted a sister—a sweet sister. May I not see her?"

"Yes, under certain conditions. There are
state reasons. I will take you to a room where
she is. You must not speak to her, nor she to
you—as yet; you may make signs, and if she

loves you she will copy them exactly; if you smile at her she will smile at you. You must not go beyond the silken cord which is stretched across your part of the room, and she will not go beyond the cord which is stretched across her part. And you must not say a word about it to any one."

The child excitedly promised obedience. The king had arranged the light in the looking-glass room—it was generally called the red room—so that it should be soft and dim. "I shall wait outside," said the king. "You must only stay for a few seconds."

So Una went in, and the king waited outside with mad humor shooting out of his eyes. Presently Una came out again.

"Oh!" she cried eagerly, "how I love her! How I *love* her. My sweetest, dearest Altera! She is far—far more beautiful than I am. And she must love me, too, because she made all the signs—and so quickly. When may I speak to her and kiss her? I am really happy now that I have Altera. Oh, she is sweet!"

Then the humor all went out of the king's eyes, and great wonder came into them. "Go away, Una, for a little while," he said. "I want to think."

He went out and stretched himself in the long grass and felt half-frightened at the thing that he had done. And a little brown snake came through the grass and bit him, and he died.

There was great lamentation in the palace. The chief counsellor, at the close of the next day, went to find Una in her own room and comfort her. She had been crying all day and her face was tear-stained. As soon as he entered, before he could say anything, she spoke:

"Have you told Altera?"

"Who is Altera?" asked the counsellor blankly.

"No, you don't understand. I thought you would not. You have the king's keys there. Give me the little silver key and follow me to the red room." The child already spoke imperiously, like a queen. "Take that taper, please. I may be able to tell you about Altera directly."

At the door of the red room Una took the taper and entered, bidding the counsellor wait outside. He left the door ajar and listened. This is what he heard:

"They told you then, sweetest Altera, and you were coming to comfort me. I love you for that. You must not cry any more, because you are so beautiful, and it spoils you. I want to kiss you and have you in my arms. Speak! Speak! It can't matter now that he is dead. See, I undo the cord—and you do so too. I put down my taper—and you put down yours.

Speak to me! Come, I can wait no longer. I must go to you. Ah! you come to me. Quickly! Quickly!"

Then there was a cry—a crash of glass—a fall—a low moan—and silence.

. . . .

"When talk sends you to sleep silence wakes you," said Yseult, with a little yawn.

"Thank you, Otho," said Rosalys.

"What made you think of that story?" asked Lilias.

"You did," I answered, and withdrew from their presence.

2—THE STORY OF THE FERRYMAN

A FEW days after I had told my first story, there began to be some little talk about the Princess Lilias. There were hints and murmurs, and the burden of them was that all would be well with her again when the prince came back. I knew that they spoke of the Prince Hilaro. He had come from over seas, from the Isle of Storm, to our court and had stayed with us for a while. I saw him often then, and yet it is hard to describe him. He was young and tall; body and soul he was made of beauty, and brightness, and strength. All his days he had lived the life of a knight and of a saint, and all the great deeds that he had done, and all his long endurances and hardships, and all high and spiritual thoughts, seemed to have given something to the beauty of his face. He was made perfect. There was no fear in him, and no vanity, and nothing that was not noble. He had no idea that he was great, and to all except himself he was kind. When he was with us, there were some who thought that he loved Lilias. I, the king's fool, had thought it. But he had gone back again to his home in the Isle of Storm, and had said nothing. None of us had supposed that Lilias loved him; she seemed above all love.

Yet now we heard that the king had left the conference and had gone on to the court in the Isle of Storm. Despatches were received, and the old ministers whispered together. Folks said that Prince Hilaro was coming again, and that all would be well when the prince came back.

One night I was bidden to come to the summer-house that the king had built for the princesses in the part of the palace gardens which was called the wilderness. The three princesses were waiting for me there. Lilias stood by the window; she was in shadow; yet once I saw her eyes, looking prayers, as it seemed, at the strewn stars, for it was a glorious, fair night. Perhaps her thoughts were for a time far away with Prince Hilaro. Yseult, with flashing eyes and lips pressed close together,

touched very softly the strings of her harp.
She made it whisper curses.   Then came a scrap
of a wild song.   Rosalys, who was seated by
her side, started a little and said:

"That is horrible, Yseult—do not sing it.
But—but—yes, I must hear the rest of it.   Go
on.   Sing!"

Yseult turned to me, instead of answering
Rosalys.   "Listen, fool," she said, "listen.
This is called the 'Song of Hate,' and I love it.
See, the symphony begins—a beautiful witch-
woman, red-lipped, starving-eyed, passionate,
looking out into the storm."   Suddenly she
began to sing.   The music was the wickedest
music I ever heard in my life.   Here are the
words:

"My eyes look out on the storm and night,
    And my heart is mad with fierce delight;
    By my spells have I worked their fate aright—
        I have worked the deaths of my brothers three.

"They took my lover from my side;
    There were flashing swords, and a voice that cried;
    At the hands of the cowards my lover died—
        Dead, dead ere the dawn they'll be!

"One's gone to sea with his merchandise;
    One's gone to war where the red flag flies;
    One sits reading, to make him wise—
        Such men are my brothers three.

11

"One for his merchandise wins gold;
 One in the battle would fain be bold;
 One learns secrets manifold—
    Dead, dead ere the dawn they'll be!

"There's storm and wreck on the sea to-night;
 There's a blade that circles swift and bright;
 There's lightning to strike with a falchion white—
    These things wait for my brothers three.

"The trader will die in storm and wrack;
 And the soldier will fall and no more come back;
 And the third will be horrible, burned and black—
    Dead, dead ere the dawn they'll be!"

Over the harp-strings, breathless and swift,
upward, upward, louder and louder leaped the
storm-music; and suddenly stopped, as though
stabbed by a quick thrust, trembled, and was
still; and out of the awful hush, slowly, like a
thing that has been crushed and hurt, crept the
melody once more—whispering, sobbing:

"Oh, my dead lover, come! I fall!
 I die, and do not hear thee call;
 I see thy face no more at all—
    Come—in this darkness come to me!

"It was for thee I wrought the spell
 That even now is working well—
 For their three lives my soul in hell—
    Dead, dead ere the dawn I'll be!"

The music had us all by the throat.   No one
spoke.   I had never heard Yseult sing so effec-

tively, so dramatically before. At the last note she rose quickly, and stood for a second swaying, with fluttering breath. Rosalys was watching her anxiously. Then like a blind woman, as if she were finding her way by instinct, with hands outstretched, Yseult made her way across the room to Lilias, and flung her arms about her waist, letting her head droop. They stood there in the shadow together against the window, and Lilias said something to her, gently, as one soothes a child. I did not hear—nor try to hear—what it was. Rosalys looked nervous questions at me. Yes, I had nearly been present at a little scene, and that was not as it should be.

Presently they left the window and sat down by Rosalys. "Otho," said Lilias, "will you tell us a story—a quiet story?"

"Yes, do, Otho," said Yseult. She had sung the spirit out of her, and there were tears in her eyes—I do not know why—I cannot understand women. She had forgotten to be scornful.

This was my story:

· · · · · · · ·

On the western side of Philistia lie the Great Marshes. Stretches of wet sand flash to a sunsetting; and there are broad sheets of water and little pools; and all is flat, and desolate, and

still. And on the outskirts of the Great Marshes runs a very wide river, tired, and sliding
slowly. There is an island in it with two tall
trees on the island where the herons build, and
further down the river is a ferry and the ferryman's cottage.

It was lonely for the ferryman, because he
had none other living with him in the cottage.
The scenery did its best to be diversified, but it
was a poor, flat thing; and he could not talk to
it, of course. Sometimes for days he would
hear no human voice, because there would be no
one going to Philistia or coming from it by way
of the Great Marshes. On those days it seemed
hard to him that the birds on their island should
be happy, or that the sun should be bright, or
that the long tremble of the moon by night
should turn the marshes to a golden dream.
Sometimes he would speak to himself:

"Why do you go on doing it? The light
will come and the darkness will follow with its
sleep, whether you live or die. And all will be
the same, whether you live or die. For if you
died another would come to row the folk across
the wide river, one who would perhaps have
wife and child to make a sweetness of this solitude. Why do you go on?"

Or he would speak to the river:

"River, why do you go on? Do you not know
what will be the end of it—the awful, limitless

sea where you will be lost, lost? Why did you come this way? Why did you not pass through the city—four miles yonder—where there are children, and love, and laughter? Poor river, you could not help yourself, just as no man can help himself. The tilt of the land for you and the set of circumstances for me; and we both go on."

On the other side of the river, nearer to Philistia, there stood a tall tower, and in the tower there hung a great bell; so that those who came from Philistia and would cross the wide river might make the bell speak. Far away on his side the ferryman could hear the bell, and would bring his boat to take the folk across.

Now one night he lay awake, obeying that wise ordinance by which the more a man wishes to sleep and forget, the more it is absolutely certain that he will lie awake and think. And suddenly he heard in the distance on the other side of the river the bell clanging irregularly.

"It is a woman," he thought to himself. Hurriedly he dressed, and pulled his heavy old boat across over the still river to the landing-stage. There was a lantern burning there all night, and by its light he saw on the lowest step a woman standing—a strange figure.

She had an imperious face, but the pride of her gray eyes and firm mouth was touched and softened by weariness and sorrow. Over her hair and shoulders she had flung something of silver and gray; her dress was white and gold, and the train of it was flung over one arm; he could see tiny silken shoes and the flash of gems on the buckles. She was splendid in the lantern light, with the screen of dark trees behind her that hid the roadway. But what did she alone by night in such attire?

She stepped into the boat, saying nothing, and seated herself in the stern of it. The ferryman, half-dazed with wonder, began to pull slowly back again with his precious cargo of gems and beauty, when he heard the sound of wheels dying away in the distance on the road that the dark trees hid. "It is the carriage that brought her," he thought. When they had reached the middle of the river, she spoke at last. Her voice was a voice to move men.

"Row no farther," she said. "Let the boat drift; and in an hour's time take me back once more to the landing-stage. My carriage will have returned, and will be waiting in the road."

He bowed his head and did as she bade him, and said nothing. With every tone of her voice and with every glance of her gray eyes the world was changing for him. And it would all be for an hour—for an hour only. She began to speak once more:

"Did I wake you? No? I was so weary of

it all. Every night in the city yonder it is the same for me—dance, and mask, and pageantry; crowds, and brilliancy, and glare, and emptiness." She laughed softly to herself; and it was to herself that she seemed to be speaking when she continued: "To-night I slipped away unnoticed. It was intolerable, it was stifling. And I thought of this wide, silent river four miles away; I thought that the quiet, the coolness, the drifting, would be sweet for an hour. Perhaps even now they are wondering—wondering." The night was sultry, and she flung off the shawl of silver and gray; the white moonlight covered her; the diamonds sparkled in her hair and on her white neck.

There was a long spell of silence, and then she made the ferryman speak of the ways of birds, of the sandy ridge a mile away, high above the sea, where the yellow poppies grew; of the legend about the ghost-moth; of his cottage; of himself. "Alone?" she said; "always alone? Almost I would that I were you. You cannot think how in the end the monotonous brightness of life wearies and hurts one." She did not know what she was doing with her words and her perfect presence. And the talk went on, broken by easy silences.

A dark thought came to the ferryman. He could not live with her, with this woman for whom he seemed to have been waiting all his

life, for one more hour. But it would not be
hard to die with her, going down under the
sliding waters. No, he would not mar what he
could not make.

And at last, as they neared the landing-stage
again, something seemed to tell her that it would
be kinder not to pay this man in the usual
way. "I want to give you something," she
said. "Let me give you a new boat; this is so
old."

He shook his head. His eyes were fixed on
the purple flowers dying in the gemmed clasp
at her breast. "May I have those flowers?" he
asked.

Amusement touched the corners of her mouth.
He was the third man who had asked her for
them that night. "You may not," she said
shortly. Two servants were waiting at the
landing-stage, and helped her from the boat.
She had grown a little angry, and she whispered
a word to one of the servants. In obedience the
man flung a couple of gold pieces half-contempt-
uously into the ferryman's boat. The ferryman murmured a word of mechanical thanks
and pulled back to the cottage. He made the
boat fast. As it lay there, the moonlight fell
on the gold pieces still lying at the bottom of
the boat.

And the ferryman went into his cottage and
threw himself once more upon his bed. "If

there is any mercy—any mercy," he cried, "I shall die this night."

He did not die; and the nights, and days, and loneliness went on as before; and nothing was changed.

.   .   .   .

As I went back alone from the summer-house to the palace, Lilias came up with me and walked a few steps by my side, in silence, down the great avenue. And then she put one hand lightly on my shoulder:

"You are not very happy, Otho, are you?" she said gently.

I tried to speak, but my voice choked me. I shook my head.

"Nor I," she said, "nor I."

3—THE STORY OF SYBIL

I WANDERED aimlessly out into that part of the gardens which was called the Wilderness. I had not been bidden to come to the princesses that night; and it seemed that by this time all within the palace were sleeping, for all the lights were out. The day had been stifling and noisy; but now beyond the palace, in the terraced gardens and right away to the stretch of sleeping hills, there were cool, quiet hours. A shy wind—red-lipped, as I fancied, from secret kisses of flowers—came stealing out, as though it had been afraid to come by day, lest it should meet people who would not understand it. I could hear the fall of the fountain, as it whispered love-stories to the ghost-stars reflected in its dark basin. Suddenly in the plantation, a little farther off, an owl hooted. It was like the cry of a mad woman. Then once more there were only murmurs—whisper of wind, and trees, and water.

Over the patient crouching hills came the moon, like a golden spirit flying slowly in its sleep. The light fell brightly on the gardens of the palace.

And now I stood at one side of a broad lawn, and on the farther side was the plantation. All day Lilias had been in my thoughts, and I knew by sympathy that she was in the night; I was not startled when I saw her come out from the darkness of yonder trees on to the lawn. She was all in white—a peaceful figure. She had seen me, and came toward me, stretching out both hands. " Otho," she said, " Otho, you too? I am glad, because I want a story. Rosalys and Yseult are sleeping, and I thought that I could not send for you because it was so late. Tell me a story to take me from my thoughts."

We walked together to an old stone seat under the trees. She sat down there, and I stretched myself on the grass at her feet, waiting to see

my story that I was to tell her. I looked out
into the night and then upward to her. The
scent of the white flowers that she wore came
down to me; almost I heard her thoughts. And
all the world seemed a mist of dreams and pictures, and she alone was real. Life was like a
tense string of a 'cello, touched steadily by the
bow, vibrating, pleading. Suddenly I became
conscious that she was speaking to me. I fancy
she was asking me if I were tired, if I would
rather not tell her a story that night.

"No, no," I said, "I see the story now."

. . . .

There was once a girl-child who had very
little luck indeed. She had six sisters all of a
larger size and of a more comely appearance
than herself, who loved her and were rather
amused at her. For she was always demurely
sad; and yet obviously wanted to be happy,
and thought a good deal about different ways to
be happy.

"I'm afraid she's not a very pretty child,"
said the eldest sister, who was a beauty. "Poor
little Sybil! she will feel that when she
grows up."

This was true. The Fates had given Sybil
short red hair, and freckles, and a curious, sal-
low little face that had lots of thoughts in it but
no dimples.

When she was quite a small child her sisters gave her a large doll which was all that mechanism and wax could be. "That's to make you happy," said the eldest sister.

"Is it?" said Sybil; "thank you." She took the large doll and squeezed its waist according to instructions, and thereout came something like a very bad quack.

"It's saying 'papa,'" exclaimed the second sister.

"Is it?" said Sybil; "thank you." Then she kissed the large doll on a portion of its face. Now the large doll was very cold and tasted very much of paint, and did not kiss her back again.

"Thank you all very much," said Sybil. "And I like you for being so kind to me. But the doll's not—not IT."

"What's IT?" asked the third sister.

"I don't know — the thing I want most badly."

"We can all of us kiss you," explained the eldest sister, "and we like kissing you, if that's IT."

Sybil shook her head. "If you couldn't kiss me—couldn't anyhow—and yet somehow did, I believe that would be something like IT."

And at this Sybil's six sisters smiled amusedly and said she was a queer child, and let her be. And years passed; and Sybil went on being demurely sad—she never grumbled; and she grew taller, and older, but not prettier. On her fourteenth birthday she had not yet found what she wanted, and did not yet know what it was. She went out into the garden and walked to an archway where the sun was blazing. Round the archway clematis grew, and one grand purple flower touched her cheek as she went under the archway. She stopped short and picked it, and held it out a little way from her in the bright sunlight.

"You *do* know me well," she said. She was sometimes rather shy in speaking her thoughts to her sisters; but to inarticulate beauty she would often speak freely. "And if I knew you as well, that would be almost—almost IT."

Then she put the flower in her dress. Her eldest sister saw it there. "I wouldn't wear purple flowers, if I were you, Sybil; you see your hair's——"

"Yes, yes—don't," said Sybil piteously. "I know—you're right—I won't wear them any more." And she gave the purple flower to her sister, whom it suited admirably. And the sister being pleased offered to kiss Sybil.

"No—not now," pleaded Sybil.

"What a quaint child you are! Why not?"

"Because—because it wouldn't make any difference," said Sybil, laughing as she went away; and she went straight upstairs to her

own room and lay down on her bed and cried
bitterly without knowing why.

Two more years passed, and many things
happened. Four of her sisters got married
and one of them died. And the one that died
was the happiest, though that has nothing to
do with the story. So Sybil was left now with
only one sister, whose name was Helen. At
sixteen years old Sybil wanted IT more than
ever, and yet she did not know what it was.
And one day she was reading some queer verses
called "Values," by a man who had failed at
verse and quite a variety of other things. And
these verses, not good enough to quote, made
some impression upon her. They told that
when work was all done and all ridiculed, when
you were left out, passed by, or even execrated,
when you saw that you had done your best and
that nobody thought it was worth having done
—you need not care if there was one—that one
—to tell you not to mind, because she knew and
understood. Sybil read these verses several
times, and it seemed to her that the man who
wrote them must have known IT.

She was not seventeen when she first knew.
She saw a man falling in love with her sister
Helen, and she saw her sister fall very much in
love with the man. And for Sybil this man
was the one—that one. The whole thing
dawned on her one evening—an evening that

she had got through somehow, she hardly knew
how. Only she was glad when the man had
gone from the house, and she had said good-
night to Helen and found refuge in her own
room.   For a time she stood before her window,
lonely, trembling, hardly daring to think.   Then
she turned to a bowl of flowers on her table and
took out one.   It was the ugliest flower there, a
rose of an unpleasant pink color, very hard and
knob-like, with hardly any fragrance.   She
chose it because it was such an ugly, forsaken
little monstrosity.   And she whispered to it all
her story—her ordinary, commonplace story—
that yet hurt her just as much as if it had been
a novelty and worth putting in a book.   "Now
go to sleep," she said, as she put the rose back
in the bowl, "and don't tell the other flowers."
She was wondering if it were possible that ugly,
deformed rose had the same kind of trouble.

In spite of trouble she slept for an hour, and
woke up to find with a kind of surprise that the
world was going on just the same.   "Yes,"
she sighed, "that will be the worst—to go on as
if nothing had happened, when it's just everything for me that has happened; and not to let
Helen see; not to let any one even guess."

And blessed are the ugly failures who have
feelings, for their days are generally long in
the land.   Sybil lived to be an old maid and
grew a shade uglier, and was thought by some

to be rather cantankerous.   She was only rather heart-broken.

.   .   .   .

Far away in the East a new day was beginning.

"Yes, yes," said Lilias, "it is hard for women who are not beautiful and yet have hearts.   It's harder always for women than for men."

We walked back together toward the palace. I wonder whether what she said was true—if such things really are harder for women.

4—THE STORY OF THE CAPTIVE

OUR good, erratic king had come back again from the Isle of Storm.   He looked as if he knew things and as if they pleased him.   But he was taken with an unusual fit of discretion and said nothing.   Sometimes I noticed Lilias looking wistfully at him, as if she had expected a message.   Yet there were the old rumors— rumors that the Prince Hilaro was coming back to us once more, for the love he had of Lilias; and that all would be well when the prince came back.

The rich summer days went by in a beautiful adagio.   By day the sun was hot and the air was still; there was a patience in everything, a waiting for something to come.   The green stalks, growing all together, were happy, yet longing; for they knew they would be golden and happier soon. The leaves of the lime-trees were passionate with innumerable bright tremblings. "Yes, we will wait," they said. "We will wait quite calmly. But, oh! to fall gently down on to the dark, fragrant earth, and to lie there in cool brown quiet until the feet of the little children pass through and make us a rustling music for their pleasure!" But in the evening the clouds were sorrowful because the sun had loved them—kissed them until they were crimson—and now he was going away. And at night in the plantation the nightingale sang, "To be beloved is the only joy; and to love is the only sorrow; but the miracle that passes music comes when that joy and sorrow meet. The silence of it is silence on fire." The frogs heard it and croaked, "Utterly morbid! utterly morbid!" They had the trained critical taste, those frogs. Yet the nightingale, who did not sing exclusively for publication, went on: "Come to me, fiery silence! Come to me now! For of sorrow, sorrow only, I am a-weary. Come to me!"

On one of these warm summer nights the princesses and I were together in the south room. The windows were open; and the moonlight came just into the room, blending curiously with the faint yellow glow from the hanging lamp. The great mastiff, that belonged

12

to Rosalys, was stretched at the feet of its mistress, asleep. Yseult lay back upon deep cushions, her hands clasped behind her head; there was generally a pretty kind of insolence in her look, but to-night her eyes seem softer. Since that night when she sang I had liked her better —for all her petulance and waywardness. And of Lilias it is not easy to speak. For although she was always beautiful, at certain times her beauty was more eloquent than at others. The gray eyes go to Paradise; her eyes to-night seemed as though already they saw within the gates.

I have often wondered that I dared to tell Lilias any stories at all.

This was the story that I told her:

.   .   .   .

"And so," said the king not unkindly, "they took you away, did they?"

He was a young king and quite new to the conquering business. His father, whom he had succeeded, had done well at it. His ministers had told him that it was among the dearest traditions of his country. So he had done a little—just a very little—conquering; and now he was trying to look at it from the point of view of the conquered. He was talking it over with one of the captives. The captive whom he had chosen for this purpose was a woman, young and most wickedly beautiful. He was a king, but he was also a man.

The king and the captive were alone together. It was a quaint room, hung with dim tapestries, lit by tapers placed in little groups. There were spots of light in the room, and corners where the shadows were deep and dark. There were rugs lying loosely on the black polished floor. The king himself was lounging carelessly in the deep window-seat; he had the curious, half-reckless look that comes from too much happiness and success. Behind him were the leaded, diamond-shaped panes of greenish glass. Old trees growing just outside stretched thin arms and tapped lightly on the glass when the wind blew; behind the trees one saw a flat country meeting a deep gray sky with a young moon in it and as many stars as it wanted. The captive had stretched herself at full length on a low couch in a recess of the room, facing the king. There was the grace of an untrained flower about her. Her hair was midnight, her eyes were all sleep and fire with long dark lashes; her lips were red. She was pale, almost dusky—no pink-and-white beauty. Her dress was scarlet and gold, a barbaric dress; but it loved her and went the way that made her most impressive. It was clasped at her breast by a strange serpent, wrought in gold, with diamond eyes that laughed to the taper-light as she breathed. One hand held a long spray of heavily scented white flowers. The other was thrust into the loose girdle of her dress; yes, it was there—a slight, curved blade, but it would suffice.

"And so they took you away?" the king said.

She turned her eyes from him and answered: "Yes, they took me away. My sister was murdered by them. All whom I loved were murdered by them. They burnt down our house and laid waste our lands. And they treated me most courteously—sweetly, kindly— and that was the cruellest thing of all." Her voice had been soft and musical; there had been no anger in it; yet there was a moment's glimpse of set white teeth between her red lips at the close of the sentence. Suddenly she remembered that her words were ill-advised; it was her plan to charm the young king to her, to win him as most women can win most men, and then at the right moment to strike with the poisoned dagger that she had hidden in her dress. "It was the king's pleasure," she added. "Shall not a king do as he will?" Her little fingers clasped firmly the graven gold that made the handle of her blade. She was surprised that the king did not speak; she had been half afraid that he would be angry with her and send her away.

"It was not my pleasure," the king said at last. "I do not make war on women. I was not there—I never knew such things were happening. But why—why should I excuse myself to you? You can never forgive me—for I should have seen that such things did not happen. I will conquer no more."

"That is true," the woman thought to herself, "I shall not forgive you, and you will certainly conquer no more." She looked straight into his eyes; the expression of his face had changed; it was troubled; he was looking fixedly at her. She began to tell him of her country; her voice was soft and alluring; with every word she drew the spell closer round him. Yes, she had made her plan well when she had based it on the fact that the king was a man.

"For the harm that I have done I will pay to the uttermost, as far as man can," said the king.

The woman smiled. "That also," she thought, "was quite true."

"But I am glad that they were kind to you," the king added. "Why was that? Yes, I remember, you can sing. They thought that I should like to hear you sing. Your name is Enid, is it not?"

"That is my name. I will sing for you, I will——" she checked herself, and made her eyes look passionate, unspeakable things. Swift as

light the passion flashed back from the eyes of
the king.   Why did she quiver under it—thrill
under it?   She explained it to herself that it
was just from the joy of vengeance.

"It was war for the sake of war," the king
said sadly.   "My ministers advised me into it.
Surely there must be something which I can do
to make amends."

And then for a long time they talked about
the war.   And all the time Enid felt that it
would have been easier for her if the king had
been somehow different.   Why was he so
gentle?   Why did he seem to want her sympathy and pity?   Worse yet—why did he almost
get them?   She found herself saying that the
cruelty of the war was not his fault—and believing it.   A chance word of the king's—he
happened to speak of "victory"—brought her
back again to her plot.   "I will do it.   I can
do it," she said to herself.   Just then the king
happened to ask if there were anything that he
could do to make her happier.

"Nothing, I think—I don't know.   It is
lonely, very lonely; and I am not one of those
that suffer it easily.   The palace is beautiful;
the whole of your kingdom is beautiful; and I
am no longer angry that you are kind to me.
But that is not enough for the happiness of a
woman.   I want more.   I want sympathy.   I
want—oh, I say too much!"

She had risen from the low couch, and stood with swimming eyes and outstretched hands. It was brilliant art—or perfect nature.

"Enid! Enid!" said the king in a low voice.

"I will sing to you," she said. She took her mandolin from a table near her and ran her fingers over it to see if it was in tune. Then she began to put out the taper-lights one by one. "It is a song that is best sung in the darkness." She knew that if she saw his face she would not be able to kill him. Then she seated herself on the couch again.

She sang the first verse. It was a love-song. The music to it was the music that takes tight hold of one. The appeal of it was irresistible. There was just enough light came through the windows to show her that the young king had sprung from his place. He came rapidly across the room to her. She flung the mandolin on one side and began to feel hurriedly for the dagger.

But already he held her hands. She was standing up now, swaying. Lights seemed to be dancing through the darkness before her eyes.

"Enid!" he was saying. "Forgive me! I love you. It is you that have conquered; I am the captive."

"No, no," she answered. "You have conquered once more. For I meant to kill you,

and now—now—I love you more than my life
—more than all the world." And the rest of
their words were whispers in the darkness—
broken with long kisses and the happiest tears.

For she had remembered that the king was a
man; but she had forgotten that she herself
was a woman.

. . . . . ' . .

"But that is quite wrong," said Yseult.
"She would have killed him first and found
out that she loved him afterward."

5—THE STORY OF AN EXPERIMENT

IT was soon after this that the betrothal of
Princess Lilias and the Prince Hilaro was announced. I know nothing of the way in which
the betrothal took place, except that Prince
Hilaro sent a messenger to our court, bearing
letters for the king and Princess Lilias. The
announcement had been constantly expected,
and yet it surprised us when it came. A change
took place in Lilias; her eyes grew wonderfully
bright and eager. There was a faint, beautiful
color in her cheeks. She walked erect, her head
a little thrown back. Great passion is only
possible to those of great spirituality. Now,
as ever before, Lilias was beyond us and above
us. Her sisters, Rosalys and Yseult, now that
she was so soon to leave them, petted her more

than ever and made much of her. Yet even at this time I knew that something was wrong with Yseult. Sometimes she seemed to me to be acting a part; sometimes she would spend whole days in solitude; sometimes she would seem almost to shrink from Lilias. But no one thought this of any importance. "Yseult is always wayward," Rosalys said to me.

Joy as well as sorrow has its insomnia, but many of these sweet summer nights Princess Lilias could not sleep, and sent for me to tell her stories. I have already said that I am condemned to die; my time is very short and I cannot write down all those stories. I knew that if any man in the world was worthy of Lilias, Hilaro was that man. He was brave and good and beautiful; rich and of high birth. And to the man that had much, much was given. And I, who had nothing, was allowed to sit at the feet of Princess Lilias and tell her stories. I would not think about it. It was too humorous; and one does not care to think about his own tragedy, when even he himself can see that that tragedy is farcical.

I am going to write now the story of the last night but one. It was expected that on the following day Prince Hilaro would sail from his own island, and would arrive by the next dawn at the court.

The king and several of the courtiers happened to have joined the princesses to listen to the story. They were all grouped together at one end of the great hall, where the lights were placed; the farther end of the hall was quite dark. Yseult had been playing to us and singing; her eyes were fixed on me, with guesses in them. I sat crouched in the shadow. I almost thought that Yseult had guessed my secret. It did not matter. Lilias did not know. When the news of her betrothal had first been announced I had put the whole thing from me and had refused to think about it; but all this day I had *had* to think about it. It came between me and everything. I could not get past it. I had a consciousness that I was mastered.

All day the air had been still, heavy, sultry; at evening the clouds drew themselves together and waited in blackness and anger. As the last notes of the music ceased, a flash of lightning, strangely bright, shone over us. The darkness at the farther end of the hall ran away from it, and for a moment let us see the dark panelling and the dim portraits in the deep frames above. The king involuntarily put his hand over his eyes and shrank back a little.

"But that was fierce!" he said.

Almost immediately the high windows began to rattle; low and quivering, then sonorous and prolonged, came the rattle of the thunder. Then followed the swift kiss of the rain. Yseult laughed and touched the harp-strings. It was the melody of " The Song of Hate " whispered. Then another flash tore at the darkness with its white fingers.

" Thank Heaven ! " said the king, " that it is to-morrow night, and not to-night, that the Prince Hilaro will be on the sea."

As he said these words it happened that I— and I alone—was closely watching the Princess Yseult. She half-started from her place, one hand moved to her throat, her color changed, and her eyes—well, there was more in them than I cared to think about.

But this much I knew, and had not known before, that Yseult loved Prince Hilaro. Under those light, wayward moods—those flashes of temper and tenderness—there had been a deep current that we had never been allowed to see. I was to learn something of its tragic intensity later on this night. I guessed even then that in some way or other Yseult knew that Prince Hilaro would be crossing the sea *that night*, and not—as the rest of us thought—on the mor-row's night. I know now, by the light of the events which followed, that while she was play-ing, singing, laughing this evening, she must have been maddened with love and jealousy.

It was quite a short story that I told this night.

. . . .

There were once two brothers of a royal house. One of them, Bertillon, was born in the spring-time; his younger brother Bruno was born eighteen months afterward in the autumn. As soon as they were old enough to do anything they both began to hate. They hated one another.

In all things they were too well matched. In appearance they were alike; in the field their prowess was equal; none could say that one was more quick-witted than the other. As they grew up their hatred increased.

"Bertillon," said Bruno one day, "if you were only a little better than I am, I could bear with you. But you are not. Your sole superiority lies in age; you have the virtue of an antique."

"Bruno," answered the elder brother, "be a little worse than I am, and I will forgive you for existing; you are only inferior in years; you inspire the same disgust as an excellent replica."

When the king, their father, died, Bertillon by reason of his superior age ascended the throne; and Bruno, supported by a small section of the province and with a hopelessly inferior army, made war upon him. In this war Bruno was defeated; and, being taken prisoner, was sentenced to death for his treason by his brother Bertillon.

"But," said Bertillon, "I will not tell you on what day you will die. You will be allowed a moderate liberty, within the prison walls; you may amuse yourself as you will; one day when you are not expecting it, when you are in the middle of some story that interests you, when you have begun to think that I must have forgiven you—the man to whom this is appointed will bring you the poisoned cup. Perhaps you will be made to drink it; and perhaps the man will only frighten you, laugh at you, and take the cup away again for a time. I shall have you watched, so that you will not be able to take your own life. I shall play with you. It will amuse me."

"There must be two to every game," said Bruno. "Nothing that you can do will make the least difference to me. You are an antique, you know, and sooner than you think your passion for being the only extant specimen will get the better of you, and you will kill me. You have not even the strength to carry out your own paltry plans."

As soon as Bruno had been removed, Bertillon turned to his councillors:

"This is a little experiment of mine. I am not really going to kill my brother Bruno at all. He will really be in just the same position as any one of us, except that he will think about it. Any one of us may die on any day, at any hour or moment; but we never think about it, and consequently it does not hurt us. Now Bruno will be asking himself every moment if he has another moment to live—if it is worth while to begin anything, since he may not be able to finish it. *He will think about it, and consequently he will go mad!*"

In three weeks' time Bruno gave in and sent a humble petition that he might be killed at once. "For," he said, "I would sooner lose my life than my reason."

"You are amusing me," was the message that Bertillon sent back.

"I shall not amuse you any more," was Bruno's reply. Nor did he. It had suddenly occurred to him that he was in no worse position than any one else; all must die, and none knows when. He resolutely put the whole thing from his mind, and lived a very cheerful, pleasant life.

But, as it happened, Bertillon, in devising this punishment, had pictured to himself rather too vividly this awful uncertainty. The thought of it had fixed its claws in his consciousness and could not be torn away. By day and night it haunted him. He constantly heard a voice warning him, "There may be but one hour between you and the hereafter."

So it happened curiously enough that it was

Bertillon, not Bruno, who went mad. Bruno succeeded him.

The only real things in this life are the things which exist solely in the imagination.

.   .   .   .

The storm had ceased. As I passed out of the great hall into the palace gardens, Lilias followed me.

" Otho," she said, " to-morrow night you must tell me another story, for Prince Hilaro will not arrive until dawn. And then—then there will be no more need for stories. I am not un-happy any longer now, Otho. You have been good to me—is there nothing that I could do for you? "

She really did not know; I wonder why.

I walked away in the direction of the coast that night. It was five miles from the palace. I felt sure that Prince Hilaro would arrive this night, and that Yseult not only knew it, but was the cause of it. I thought it better to be there, for I had seen for one second into Yseult's real nature, and I hardly knew what she would do. On reaching the cliff I could see nothing, and being very tired, I flung myself down in the wet, long grasses that met over my head, and slept. It was gray dawn when I was wakened by hearing voices.

They were the voices of Prince Hilaro and Yseult. Raising myself slightly, I saw that they were standing on the cliff edge a few yards from me.

"I did as your letter asked," he was saying. "I came a day sooner, and met you here alone, secretly, at this hour as you wished, because you said it was necessary for the happiness of Lilias. And now you have nothing to say but to ask me if I love her?"

Yseult laughed lightly. "I love Lilias better than any in the world—save one. I would give her my life, my soul, everything—except one."

I crept a little closer, for I knew now what she would do. But it came sooner than I had thought.

"What is that one?"

"You, Hilaro!" she cried, suddenly letting her voice go as it would—"you, whom I love—and *hate!*"

With these words she thrust suddenly at him with a short, curved knife that she had held concealed. The blade went into his throat, and he staggered backward over the cliff. I was just in time to drag her back from flinging herself after him.

"Otho! Otho!" she said, panting for breath, "I have killed him. Let me go."

I took her backward a few paces from the cliff

edge and looked into her eyes. "Now you may go," I said; "kill yourself also."

She swayed and fell face downward in the grass, moaning: "I dare not die! Otho, I dare not die!" I had seen that in her eyes.

And there, after a little while, in the gray dawn I showed her what she must do.

6—THE STORY OF A PICTURE

I HAD but a short time in which to persuade Yseult to agree to the plan which I had formed; for it was necessary that we should both return to the palace and enter it unobserved while all were still sleeping. She was shaken with excitement, terror, fever; but she had no remorse.

At last I made her believe all that was necessary—that the murder of Hilaro had been committed in an hour of madness, and was not really murder; that Lilias must never know that the sister she loved had killed the man she loved; and that if I took the guilt and paid the penalty it would be best.

"But," said Yseult, "if I take your life to save mine, that will be murder indeed."

I forget what lie I told her in answer to this. But I persuaded her. She clung desperately to life. As we returned she grew quite calm, and was far more ready and skilful than I in arranging the details of the plan. I could not think

13

very well. I was tired out—soul and body—
and wanted to sleep. After a time, I just heard
her speaking without understanding what she
said.

When I got to my own room I slept easily
and dreamlessly. It was late in the day when
I woke again, and the setting sun was shining
in at my windows. Underneath them I heard
the voices of the three princesses as they passed
down the steps of the terrace. Rosalys was
laughing. So the body, shattered and spoiled
by the knife and the jagged rocks, had not yet
been found. The prince's companions were to
come ashore to-night, and had been ordered to
meet him on the cliff. Yseult had told me this.
They would find the body and bring it with
them to the palace.

That night I told a story to the three princesses
under the open sky, on a broad lawn in the palace
gardens. I knew that Lilias had chosen this
spot because from it she could see the road to the
palace, bending with a broad, white curve in the
moonlight. She thought that her lover would
come by that way before the dawn, with music
and gladness, strong and beautiful, with the
retinue from his court attending him. She
wished to be among the first to welcome him
and do him honor. Her eyes were bright with
ecstasy.

Both Rosalys and Lilias were very affection-

ate with Yseult that night. "Poor Yseult has
hardly spoken a word all day," said Rosalys.
"You are not ill, Yseult, are you? "

She shook her head sadly. She was acting
her part to perfection.

"And now tell your story," said Rosalys,
turning to me. "There will be little sleep to-
night for any of us. All within the palace are
busy preparing to receive the prince. There is
a watchman on the towers who will see the
lights that the prince's company will carry as
they come down yonder road, and will give the
signal of his approach. Then all the palace will
be lit up, and there will be music and revelry."

So I began my story.

.   .   .   .

As generally happens, these two people, who
had not long been married, were coming down
from the heights. He, the poet, felt almost
with regret the vanishing of that fierce sense of
exaltation which had been his when he first
knew that this woman loved him, and trembled
in knowing it. He could recall old days, before
he had spoken, when he had weighed each
chance word that he heard from her and drawn
from it ecstasy or despair, when every moment
that he did not see her had seemed to him blank
and wasted. He had not ceased to love her
now; only there were no more discoveries to

make and nothing more to say, and vain repetition had drawn all the sweetness from sweet
love-words. It was quiet, placid love. He was
so sure of it that he could put it from his mind
for a little. There had been days, he remembered, when he had been unable to write or read
for thinking of one thing; there had been nights
when he had been unable to sleep for continued
thinking of one thing. They never came now.
She felt the change too. She had fallen in love
with the poet—almost with the reputation; she
had married the man. The days of fears, of
hopes, of secrets, of idealizing were over. She
loved him still, but without any illusions, without honestly thinking herself honored by his
love. He had just that little kink in the brain,
just that tiny turn of the temperament, which
makes the difference between the poet and the
ordinary man; but in most things he was only
ordinary. And their love was becoming ordinary too. They no longer felt that all the rest of
the world lay fathomless depths below them; they
no longer felt angry with all other people for their
gross impertinence in existing; on the contrary,
they were rather pleased when some of the rest
of the world came to see them. It made a
change.

And yet they loved one another—in the ordinary, quiet way—until that fateful time
when he had her portrait painted by Raoul. A

portrait by Raoul was generally a revelation of the person painted. "That is like my son," a woman said, looking at his portrait by Raoul; "but there is a look in the face which my son never has—it is the look of a murderer." Three years afterward, at her son's execution, she remembered that she had said that. "It's quite true," a girl said to herself, looking at her own portrait by Raoul, "but I had never told any one—how did he know?" It was acknowledged that he was the greatest portrait painter of his time and country—if he would only give up playing little tricks to amuse himself. He was also accused of laziness; and it is certain that he did not devote himself now, as he had done in his younger days, wholly to art. He had taken up with sundry curious studies, and his success had made him melancholy, taciturn, sardonical. He was middle-aged, unmarried, and rather displeasing in manner. When he had finished the portrait of the poet's wife, he smiled. Raoul seldom smiled, but the poet's wife had interested him, and he had just made a little experiment.

For a few weeks he heard nothing, and then the woman came to his studio, attended only by one servant, who carried the portrait. At her orders the man put the portrait down and left her alone with Raoul.

"Raoul," she said, "my husband is away,

and I want you to alter your portrait of me before he returns."

Raoul did not seem surprised. He hummed a fragment of a tune and glanced at her from head to foot.

"Why have you been crying?" he asked bluntly.

"I have not been crying."

The artist shrugged his shoulders and went on humming his tune. Suddenly he stopped. "If you tell me lies——" he began. Then he stopped again, for there was no doubt that the woman was crying now. He sat down and waited patiently; she told a strange story in between her sobs.

In brief, she said that her husband had, ever since the arrival of the portrait, ceased to love her. He had been absolutely cold to her, shunned her society, had never even spoken to her if he could avoid it. "But," she said, "he has fallen wildly in love with my portrait. All day he keeps it before him. He cares for nothing but to look at it. It is an absurdity—a madness; but it makes me wretched, for I never loved him so much in my life before. Oh, it is brutal of you to make me tell you this! What is it? What have you put into the portrait that I have not got?"

"Nothing," replied Raoul, "absolutely noth-

ing. I have simply left something out. I have
·painted you as though you had never loved and
would not love. He is a poet and is chiefly
attracted by the unattainable."

"They told me that in the portrait I looked
too cold."

"Too cold? Yes, that is one sign—one very
little sign, but it is not all, or nearly all. What
I have done is not merely a trick of expression.
They do not understand—these people. But
your husband is a poet—understands more than
he can explain."

"Will you alter it?"

"No, I should spoil it. Not that I care for
art—except as a means to mastery. Mastery
is what I want—to make people do things, feel
things, see things, just as I want—to get a grip
of people without their knowing how."

He looked at her again, very curiously. Then
he took the portrait to the light and carefully
examined it. "Ah!" he exclaimed under his
breath. Then he turned to the woman.

"Go away. You shall have the portrait this
evening, and your husband will soon give up
loving it. You may take my word for it. I
have changed my mind."

As soon as she had gone he went from his
studio to a room which was fitted as a labora-
tory, and returned with a little bottle containing

some colorless oily stuff. He began to work, using great precautions. Then he sent the portrait back.

The poet's wife hung the picture once more in her husband's study in its usual place, and lit the candles that stood below it. She could see that the lips in the portrait had been just touched, but she could not see that any difference had been made. Then she went to bed.

Later at night she heard her husband return to the house. The door of his study slammed, and then all the house was quiet. She waited for hours, and he did not come upstairs. At last, in the dawn, she could bear the suspense no longer, but arose and went down to the study. She knocked, but there was no answer. She thought that he might be asleep, and opened the door softly. The candles were flaring, yellow and ghastly in the gray dawn, lighting up the little picture of her own loveless face.

The poet lay in an ugly attitude, as though he had fallen, on the floor beneath the picture. His lips were white, save in just one place where there was a curious scarlet stain; and his eyes——

.   .   .   .

"Otho, stop! stop!" cried Yseult. We were all startled a little at the suddenness of it. For

a moment I was doubtful, and then I saw that
all was right, that she was just carrying out
the plan. "I can bear it no longer," she went
on, turning to Lilias; "Lilias, dearest Lilias, I
must tell you. Hilaro will not come to you to-
night. He will never come to you any more.
He is dead."

"What are you saying? What do you
mean?" said Rosalys excitedly. Lilias said
nothing. She was staring blankly at the white
curve of the road.

"This morning at dawn I was on the cliff
edge. Otho and Prince Hilaro stood there together. And as I watched, hidden, Otho drew
a knife and stabbed the prince in the throat,
and flung him over the cliff."

She spoke boldly, defiantly, dramatically. As
she was speaking, I saw lights appear in the distance on the road, and knew that they were bringing the body of the dead prince. Lilias saw
them, and with a low cry fell forward on the
grass fainting. The watchman on the tower saw
them too, and gave his signal. Immediately
the whole palace was lit up, and the doors were
flung open, and the musicians stationed there
began a joyful triumphant march.

"I will go and stop the music and——" Yseult
paused, then hastened into the palace.

And Rosalys said to me, "Why do you stand

there, Otho, with staring eyes, doing nothing?
Deny it! I command you to deny it."

" It is true!" I answered.

. . . .

And so all ends happily—for me, at least.
There was a trial—a matter of form, since both
accuser and accused were agreed. To have lived
on would have been sad enough; but to die is
easy. I have often wondered why those who
would write or tell a pathetic story will make
it end with death. To have endured the greatest sorrow and still to live is sad indeed. Death
can be very happy. Only I would that by my
death I could bring back Hilaro to life! Oh,
my Princess Lilias, I have at least saved you
one thing—you can still love your sister Yseult!
Sooner or later I think that you will make her
good like yourself. Indeed, she was good but
for that night of madness; and there are things
which we cannot control at all—we cannot say
that we will love this and not that. It is as it
comes. No man thinking of his own love-story
can well believe in his own free-will. I know
that Princess Lilias will not lose her reason nor
take her life; after some months she will try
to speak and smile once more; she will, most
pathetically, interest herself in the lives of
others. But she will never forget, and memory

will soon wear out her strength. I have heard no more of the princesses. I have written all this in the week between my sentence and my death. I am told nothing, and I can only wonder.

But it is late—late at night—and to-morrow there will be no more wonder of any kind, and no more trouble, and no more vain longing.

THE END.

TESS OF THE D'URBERVILLES.

A Pure Woman, Faithfully Presented. By THOMAS HARDY, author of "The Woodlanders," "A Laodicean," etc. Illustrated. Post 8vo, Cloth, Ornamental, $1 50. *New Edition, revised and considerably expanded by the author, according to the latest English edition.*

A remarkably fine and moving story. It is marked by all those qualities of genius which we are accustomed to associate with the work of Mr. Hardy. It is full of poetry of incident and phrase. . . . A great story. Nobody should miss it.—*N. Y. Sun.*

In "Tess of the D'Urbervilles" Thomas Hardy exhibits the strongest, and in some respects the best, piece of literary work that has ever left his pen.—*Philadelphia Ledger.*

One of the few great novels of the century.—*N. Y. Mail and Express.*

Not only by far the best work Mr. Hardy has done; it is one of the strongest novels that have appeared for a long time. . . . A more tragic or powerfully moving story than that of Tess lives not in fiction; and the pity of it is heightened by the exquisite pastoral scenes in which it is mainly set. . . . The book is full of suggestion on questions which have never agitated men's minds more than at the present time. . . . It is certainly a masterpiece, and one upon which the reputation of the author may safely rest.—*N. Y. Tribune.*

Mr. Hardy has written a novel that is not only good, but great. . . . "Tess of the D'Urbervilles" is well in front of Mr. Hardy's previous work, and is destined, there can be no doubt, to rank high among the achievements of Victorian novelists.—*Athenæum,* London.

The best English novel that has appeared for many a day. . . . The book is the most ingeniously constructed and artistically developed that has been produced by an English novelist since George Eliot's time.—*Philadelphia Bulletin.*

Powerful and strange in design, splendid and terrible in execution, this story brands itself upon the mind as with the touch of incandescent iron.—*Academy,* London.

PUBLISHED BY HARPER & BROTHERS, N. Y.

☞ *The above work is for sale by all booksellers, or will be sent by the publishers, postage prepaid, to any part of the United States, Canada, or Mexico, on receipt of price.*

W. D. HOWELLS.

THE QUALITY OF MERCY. A Novel. 12mo, Cloth, $1 50.

AN IMPERATIVE DUTY. A Novel. 12mo, Cloth, $1 00.

THE SHADOW OF A DREAM. A Story. 12mo, Cloth, $1 00; Paper, 50 cents.

A HAZARD OF NEW FORTUNES. A Novel. 12mo, Cloth, 2 vols., $2 00; Paper, Illustrated, $1 00.

ANNIE KILBURN. A Novel. 12mo, Cloth, $1 50; Paper, 75 cents.

APRIL HOPES. A Novel. 12mo, Cloth, $1 50; Paper, 75 cents.

MODERN ITALIAN POETS. Essays and Versions. With Portraits. 12mo, Half Cloth, $2 00.

CRITICISM AND FICTION. With Portrait. 16mo, Cloth, Ornamental, $1 00.

A BOY'S TOWN. Illustrated. Post 8vo, Cloth, Ornamental, $1 25.

THE MOUSE-TRAP, AND OTHER FARCES. Illustrated. 12mo, Cloth, $1 00.

THE ALBANY DEPOT. A Farce. Illustrated. Small 16mo, Cloth, Ornamental, 50 cents.

THE GARROTERS. A Farce. Small 16mo, Cloth, 50 cents.

PUBLISHED BY HARPER & BROTHERS, NEW YORK.

☞ *The above works will be sent by mail, postage prepaid, to any part of the United States, Canada, or Mexico, on receipt of the price.*

CHARLES DUDLEY WARNER.

By CONSTANCE F. WOOLSON.

BY MARY E. WILKINS.

A NEW ENGLAND NUN, and Other Stories. 16mo, Cloth, Ornamental, $1 25.

A HUMBLE ROMANCE, and Other Stories. 16mo, Cloth, Extra, $1 25.

Only an artistic hand could have written these stories, and they will make delightful reading.—*Evangelist*, N. Y.

The simplicity, purity, and quaintness of these stories set them apart in a niche of distinction where they have no rivals.—*Literary World*, Boston.

The reader who buys this book and reads it will find treble his money's worth in every one of the delightful stories.—*Chicago Journal*.

Miss Wilkins is a writer who has a gift for the rare art of creating the short story which shall be a character study and a bit of graphic picturing in one ; and all who enjoy the bright and fascinating short story will welcome this volume.—*Boston Traveller*.

The author has the unusual gift of writing a short story which is complete in itself, having a real *beginning*, a *middle*, and an *end*. The volume is an excellent one.—*Observer*, N. Y.

A gallery of striking studies in the humblest quarters of American country life. No one has dealt with this kind of life better than Miss Wilkins. Nowhere are there to be found such faithful, delicately drawn, sympathetic, tenderly humorous pictures.—*N. Y. Tribune*.

The charm of Miss Wilkins's stories is in her intimate acquaintance and comprehension of humble life, and the sweet human interest she feels and makes her readers partake of, in the simple, common, homely people she draws.—*Springfield Republican*.

There is no attempt at fine writing or structural effect, but the tender treatment of the sympathies, emotions, and passions of no very extraordinary people gives to these little stories a pathos and human feeling quite their own.—*N. Y. Commercial Advertiser*.

The author has given us studies from real life which must be the result of a lifetime of patient, sympathetic observation. . . . No one has done the same kind of work so lovingly and so well.—*Christian Register*, Boston.

PUBLISHED BY HARPER & BROTHERS, NEW YORK.

☞ *The above works sent by mail, postage prepaid, to any part of the United States, Canada, or Mexico, on receipt of the price.*

SEVEN DREAMERS.

A Collection of Seven Stories. By ANNIE TRUMBULL
SLOSSON. pp. 286. Post 8vo, Cloth, Ornamental,
$1 25.

A charming collection of character sketches and stories
—humorous, pathetic, and romantic—of New England
country life. The volume includes "How Faith Came
and Went," "Botany Bay," "Aunt Randy," "Fishin'
Jimmy," "Butterneggs," "Deacon Pheby's Selfish Nat-
ur'," and "A Speakin' Ghost."

They are of the best sort of "dialect" stories, full of humor
and quaint conceits. Gathered in a volume, with a frontispiece
which is a wonderful character sketch, they make one of the
best contributions to the light literature of this season.—*Observer*, N. Y.

Stories told with much skill, tenderness, and kindliness, so
much so that the reader is drawn powerfully towards the poor
subjects of them, and soon learns to join the author in looking
behind their peculiarities and recognizing special spiritual gifts
in them.—*N. Y. Tribune.*

These stories are of such originality, abounding in deep pathos and tenderness, that one finds himself in perfect accord
with the writer as he reads of the hallucinations of these heroes.—*Watchman*, Boston.

Dreamers of a singular kind, they affect us like the inhabitants of allegories—a walk of literary art in which we have had
no master since the pen dropped from the faint and feeble fingers of Hawthorne, and which seems native to Mrs. Slosson.—
N. Y. Mail and Express.

The sweetness, the spiciness, the aromatic taste of the forest
has crept into these tales.—*Philadelphia Ledger.*

PUBLISHED BY HARPER & BROTHERS, NEW YORK.

☞ *The above work will be sent by mail, postage prepaid, to any part
of the United States, Canada, or Mexico, on receipt of the price.*

BEN-HUR:

A TALE OF THE CHRIST. By LEW. WALLACE. 16mo, Cloth, $1 50; Half Leather, $2 00; Three-quarter Leather, $2 50; Half Calf, $3 00; Full Leather, $3 50; Three-quarter Crushed Levant, $4 00.—GARFIELD EDITION. 2 volumes. Illustrated with twenty full-page photogravures. Over 1,000 illustrations as marginal drawings by WILLIAM MARTIN JOHNSON. Crown 8vo, Silk and Gold, Uncut Edges and Gilt Tops, $7 00. (*In a Gladstone box.*)

Anything so startling, new, and distinctive as the leading feature of this romance does not often appear in works of fiction. . . . Some of Mr. Wallace's writing is remarkable for its pathetic eloquence. The scenes described in the New Testament are rewritten with the power and skill of an accomplished master of style.—*N. Y. Times.*

Its real basis is a description of the life of the Jews and Romans at the beginning of the Christian era, and this is both forcible and brilliant . . . We are carried through a surprising variety of scenes; we witness a sea-fight, a chariot-race, the internal economy of a Roman galley, domestic interiors at Antioch, at Jerusalem, and among the tribes of the desert; palaces, prisons, the haunts of dissipated Roman youth, the houses of pious families of Israel. There is plenty of exciting incident; everything is animated, vivid, and glowing.—*N. Y. Tribune.*

It is full of poetic beauty, as though born of an Eastern sage, and there is sufficient of Oriental customs, geography, nomenclature, etc., to greatly strengthen the semblance.—*Boston Commonwealth.*

"Ben-Hur" is interesting, and its characterization is fine and strong. Meanwhile it evinces careful study of the period in which the scene is laid, and will help those who read it with reasonable attention to realize the nature and conditions of Hebrew life in Jerusalem and Roman life at Antioch at the time of our Saviour's advent.—*Examiner, N. Y.*

The book is one of unquestionable power, and will be read with unwonted interest by many readers who are weary of the conventional novel and romance.—*Boston Journal.*

PUBLISHED BY HARPER & BROTHERS, NEW YORK.

☞ *The above work sent by mail, postage prepaid, to any part of the United States, Canada, or Mexico, on receipt of the price.*

BY MRS. BURTON HARRISON.

BAR HARBOR DAYS. A Tale of Mount Desert. Illustrated by Fenn and Hyde. 16mo, Cloth, $1 25.

A bright story of life at Mount Desert. . . . It is exceedingly well done, and the scenery, the ways of the people, and the social methods of the rusticators lend interest to the book.—*Christian Advocate*, N. Y.

The book is bright and readable.—*Courier*, Boston.

A delightful book about Mount Desert, its summer inhabitants, their sayings and doings.—*N. Y. Sun.*

One of the most attractive books of the season, and will be in great demand by readers who wish an original, captivating summer idyl.—*Hartford Post.*

HELEN TROY 16mo, Cloth, $1 00.

It is a breezy little society novel, with a pretty plot and a number of capitally drawn characters. . . . It is always bright, fresh, and entertaining, and has an element of naturalness that is particularly pleasing. The descriptions are very spirited, the conversations are full of point and often genuinely witty, and the tone of the whole is both refined and delicate.—*Saturday Evening Gazette*, Boston.

The book is written with exceeding cleverness, and abounds in delightful little pictures.—*The Critic*, N. Y.

Mrs. Harrison's style is crisp, epigrammatic, piquant; she shades her characters artistically, paints from real life, and, without hurrying the reader along, never lets her story drag. . . . The merit of the work lies in the fidelity of its portraiture and the felicity of its utterance.—*N. Y. Herald.*

GOLDEN ROD . AN IDYL OF MOUNT DESERT. 32mo, Paper, 25 cents; Cloth, 40 cents.

A very sweet little story of a successful courtship, wrought into a charming description of scenery and life on Mount Desert.—*Springfield* (Ill.) *State Journal.*

This is a most charming summer story—"An Idyl of Mount Desert"—the mere reading of which makes you long to be there, and to feel sure you will find the delightful people, and just in the particular nooks, you have been reading about. — *Galesburg* (Ill.) *Republican Register.*

PUBLISHED BY HARPER & BROTHERS, NEW YORK.

☞ *The above works sent by mail, postage prepaid, to any part of the United States or Canada, on receipt of the price.*

THE CAPTAIN OF THE JANIZARIES.

A Tale of the Times of Scanderbeg and the Fall of
Constantinople.   By JAMES M. LUDLOW, D.D.,
Litt.D.   16mo, Cloth, $1 50.

The author writes clearly and easily; his descriptions are
often of much brilliancy, while the whole setting of the story is
of that rich Oriental character which fires the fancy.—*Boston
Courier.*

Strong in its central historical character, abounding in incident, rapid and stirring in action, animated and often brilliant
in style.—*Christian Union, N. Y.*

Something new and striking interests us in almost every chapter.   The peasantry of the Balkans, the training and govern-
ment of the Janizaries, the interior of Christian and Moslem
camps, the horrors of raids and battles, the violence of the Sul-
tan, the tricks of spies, the exploits of heroes, engage Mr. Ludlow's fluent pen.—*N. Y. Tribune.*

Dr. Ludlow's style is a constant reminder of Walter Scott,
and the book is to retain a permanent place in literature.—*Observer, N. Y.*

An altogether admirable piece of work—picturesque, truthful,
and dramatic.—*Newark Advertiser.*

A most romantic, enjoyable tale. . . . As affording views of
inner life in the East as long ago as the middle of the fifteenth
century, this tale ought to have a charm for many; but it is
full enough of incident, wherever the theatre of its action might
be found, to do this.—*Troy Press.*

The author has used his material with skill, weaving the facts
of history into a story crowded with stirring incidents and un-
expected situations, and a golden thread of love-making, under
extreme difficulties, runs through the narrative to a happy issue.
—*Examiner, N. Y.*

One of the strongest and most fascinating historical novels of
the last quarter of a century.—*Boston Pilot.*

PUBLISHED BY HARPER & BROTHERS, NEW YORK.

☞ *The above work sent by mail, postage prepaid, to any part of the
United States, Canada, or Mexico, on receipt of the price.*

A KING OF TYRE.

A Tale of the Times of Ezra and Nehemiah. By JAMES M. LUDLOW, D.D. 16mo, Cloth, Ornamental, $1 00.

The picture of the life and manners of that far-away period is carefully and artistically drawn, the plot is full of interest, and the whole treatment of the subject is strikingly original, and there is a dramatic intensity in the story which will at once remind the reader of "Ben-Hur."—*Boston Traveller.*

It is altogether a fresh and enjoyable tale, strong in its situations and stirring in its actions.—*Cincinnati Commercial-Gazette.*

Another distinct success in the field of historical fiction. . . . Must be unhesitatingly set down as a highly satisfactory performance.—*Boston Beacon.*

In "A King of Tyre" we live and move amid old ideas, old superstitions, and an extinct civilization. But this vanished order of things the author has pierced to the core, and laid bare the human heart that animates it all. When we say that his tale is interesting, that it is satisfying, that it is dramatically conclusive, we give it high praise, yet we give it deliberately, and are convinced that the opinion of all intelligent readers will confirm the verdict.—*Churchman*, N. Y.

Vivid with the richness of Oriental habits and customs, and the weird accompaniments of pagan worship, this tale of the times after the return of the Hebrews to their own land, will hold the attention of the reader with unflagging interest. Its development shows marked ability and skill. There is an historical basis to the story which gives it additional attraction.—*Living Church*, Chicago.

Will enhance the reputation of the author, and can be welcomed as not only a novel of absorbing interest, but a faithful study and portraiture of an eventful historical period.—*Christian Intelligencer*, N. Y.

PUBLISHED BY HARPER & BROTHERS, NEW YORK.

☞ HARPER & BROTHERS *will send the above work by mail, postage prepaid, to any part of the United States, Canada, or Mexico, on receipt of the price.*

TWO USEFUL HANDBOOKS.

EVERYBODY'S WRITING-DESK BOOK. By CHARLES NISBET and DON LEMON. Revised and Edited by JAMES BALDWIN, Ph.D. Square 16mo, Cloth, Ornamental, $1 00.

This little book is at once a guide and a friend. . . . The claim that the work will be found to comprise in one handy volume all needful instruction and guidance on all questions connected with writing can readily be admitted.—*Philadelphia Record.*

An excellent little manual of grammar, composition, etc., intended "for the service of all who write." . . . This is a thoroughly helpful and convenient book of reference.—*Chicago Tribune.*

A capital book for the student. Its rules for composition, grammar, and punctuation are simple and clear, and well calculated to start the student to thinking. . . . It is an excellent book for the pocket or the satchel.—*Chicago Inter-Ocean.*

EVERYBODY'S POCKET CYCLOPÆDIA of Things Worth Knowing, Things Difficult to Remember, and Tables of Reference. Square 16mo, Cloth, 75 cents.

The little book is really a fascinating storehouse of " things worth knowing " and easily discovered by reference to its twenty-five-page index.—*Critic,* N. Y.

An admirable little mentor in the thousand and one things that are forever eluding memory—things that we *ought* to know in every pursuit of life.—*Presbyterian,* Philadelphia.

It is remarkable how many "things worth knowing and things difficult to remember" are here crowded into small space. He is an exceptionally curious person who cannot here gratify his curiosity.—*N. Y. Sun.*

PUBLISHED BY HARPER & BROTHERS, NEW YORK.

☞ *The above works are for sale by all booksellers, or will be sent by the publishers, postage prepaid, to any part of the United States, Canada, or Mexico, on receipt of the price.*